WILD CHILD

WILD HEART MOUNTAIN: WILD RIDERS MC
BOOK TEN

SADIE KING

LET'S BE BESTIES!

A few times a month I send out an email with new releases, special deals and sneak peeks of what I'm working on. If you want to get on the list I'd love to meet you!

When you join you'll get access to all my bonus content which includes a couple of free short and steamy romances plus bonus scenes for selected books.

Sign up here:
authorsadieking.com/bonus-scenes

WILD RIDERS MC

AN INTRODUCTION

Welcome to Wild Heart Mountain home of the Wild Riders MC.

If you love damaged heroes and curvy girl romance, then you'll love the Wild Riders MC.

This group of ex-military bikers fall hard and fall fast when they encounter the curvy women who heal their hearts.

Expect forbidden love, age gap, forced proximity, fake relationships, single dads, single moms and off-limits love with protective heroes who will do anything for the women they love.

Spend some time with Wild Heart Mountain's Wild Riders MC, the MC that's all heart.

Let me introduce you to the members...

Ex-military buddies **Raiden, Quentin and Travis** formed the Wild Riders MC when they got out of the military and wanted to create a place for veterans who love to ride.

They set up their headquarters in a compound on the side of Wild Heart Mountain.

Travis, whose road name is Hops, runs the Wild Taste Bar and Restaurant, and secretly crushes on his best friend's sister.

Quentin, also known as Barrels, runs the award-winning Wild Taste Brewery located out the back of the restaurant. He was a First Class Sargent in the army and you wouldn't want to cross him. Especially where his little sister is concerned...

Colter, or Vintage, is a motorbike mechanic and runs the bike shop. He collects old bikes and loves all things vintage especially the bubbly Danni and her 1950's curves.

Calvin also known as Badge, is the local Sheriff and his uptight views that are shaped by loss.

Joseph, or Lone Star is a recluse whose military experiences have given him a distaste for humanity.

Grant goes by Snips. He's the local barber and a single dad.

Arlo earns the road name Prince because of his charming and personable nature. He loves getting under the skin of Maggie, the shy pastry chef.

Davis begins the series as a prospect. Younger than most of the other men, he came out of the military with diminished hearing. His hearing aids keeps make him shy with women and he keeps himself hidden away.

Luke becomes a prospect after Raiden finds him drinking himself to oblivion in a strip joint. A wheelchair user since he lost both his legs in Afghanistan, Luke finds new purpose with the MC, but can he find love?

Specs would rather read a book than talk to anyone.

Bit Rate is a grumpy single dad widower in need of a nanny.

Judge is a military lawyer and always does the right thing until he meets the curvy woman who makes him question his world view.

Marcus goes by Wood because his family own the local sawmill and it's his medium of choice. He channels his PTSD into his art, creating sculptures that attract the attention of an arts journalist from the city.

On the other side of Wild Heart Mountain is a town called Hope and nestled in the hills is the Emerald Heart

Resort. During the summer, it's a popular destination for tourists and in winter, they come for the ski season. Perfect for a snowed in romance…

Stay awhile in Wild Heart Mountain and explore the other series set here.

Wild Heart Mountain: Military Heroes
Wild Heart Mountain: Mountain Heroes
Temptation
A Runaway Bride for Christmas
A Secret Baby for Christmas

WILD CHILD

She's the MC President's daughter, she's off limits, we're on a road trip together, and there's only one bed!

Charlie is spontaneous and wild. She's utterly gorgeous and intent on contradicting everything I say.

She frustrates the heck out of me and turns me on in equal measure.

I shouldn't fall for the feisty MC President's daughter.

She's off limits and fifteen years younger than me.

I'm ex-military and stuck in my ways; she's a free spirit who follows her heart.

We're opposites in every way.

But when we're stuck on a road trip together and there's only one bed, I don't know how long my defenses will hold…

Wild Child is a forbidden love, age gap, forced proximity, steamy romance novella featuring an ex-military biker and the curvy younger woman who's off limits.

www.authorsadieking.com

1

QUENTIN

*C*harlie expertly weaves her way through the crowd with the drinks tray above her head. I lose her behind a man in a banana suit, and my neck strains until her shock of pink hair becomes visible at the far end of the restaurant.

She stops at a high table in the corner, and a male cheer erupts as she sets drinks down on the table. I can't see what they're cheering at, and it better just be the drinks and not their waitress.

A young man with scruffy hair who's wearing a cape leans toward Charlie and says something to her. He's leaning in close, too close.

My blood heats, and I push off from the bar. The banana suit man chooses that moment to sashay across the space between the tables and the bar. He's got his hands in the air and wiggles his banana-clad butt in time to the music. He's joined by a man dressed as a Smurf.

I hate bachelor parties. I don't know why we do them,

but Travis assures me they're good for business. I put it on my mental agenda to bring up with Raiden, the club president, when he gets back.

They come here for the craft beer tasting and brewery tour, but they end up drunk and harassing my waitresses.

Charlie throws her head back and laughs at something the customer has said. I stop in my tracks.

Charlie doesn't look harassed judging by the way she's smiling and chatting with the men in the corner.

My fists clench. Raiden asked me to keep an eye on his daughter while he's away. But it's a hard job when she's our best waitress and likes the attention, walking a fine line between talking with the customers and flirting with them.

I almost want one to put a hand on her so I have a reason to kick them all out.

But the men remain annoyingly respectful.

"We're ready when you are, VP."

I turn to Travis, and he chuckles at the scowl on my face.

"We gotta stop the bachelor parties."

"Why?" He generally doesn't see anything wrong with this situation. "The lunch crowd has gone, and there are no bookings until dinner. The tour bus will drive them back to the resort in another hour. It's easy money."

He's not wrong there. But we're a biker's bar on the side of the mountain, not a nightclub.

"There's a banana in my bar, man."

He chuckles. "I hear ya. Maybe we need boundaries."

Technically, the running of the Wild Taste Bar and Restaurant is Travis's responsibility, and I manage the brewery out back. But both businesses are under the same umbrella of the Wild Riders MC, and we have a reputation to protect.

We're a stop on a tourist day package that leaves from the Emerald Heart Resort. Our brewery tour and tasting is one of the stops, but Travis somehow thought adding a bachelor party special was a good idea. It's not. I've got a banana and a Smurf dancing in my bar.

"No fancy dress, and the minivan leaves an hour earlier than whatever time you have arranged with the resort. Once the tour and tasting is over, they can go back and party at the White Out."

Travis frowns. "The marketing is supposed to put off the rowdy lot."

We position ourselves as a craft brewery, and our marketing is aimed at a sophisticated bachelor party. If there is such a thing.

"The pricing is for the upmarket crowd," says Travis

"They're the worst," I mutter.

Travis chuckles, not committing to anything.

He lays a hand on my shoulder. "The men are waiting."

Davis is behind the bar for the afternoon, and I lean against it and give him a stern look.

"Keep an eye on Charlie, and if any of these men lay so much as a finger on her, they're all out."

He nods, and with a final glance at the bobbing pink head in the corner, I head out of the bar. Down the corridor are our club rooms, and the men are waiting in the main meeting room.

It's a Saturday afternoon, and I've called them together for an emergency meeting.

But my men don't grumble. They're all ex-military, and they know when duty calls you answer.

My gaze scans the room, taking in the few absences. Hazel is sick, and Marcus won't leave her side. Lone Star has a sick kid, but he's linked in via video call. Snip's little girl has gone down with it too. There's a tummy bug going around and half the kids have it, which is a problem.

"Thanks for coming in, guys."

I take a seat at the head of the table and pick up the gavel. It's heavy and doesn't feel right in my hand. I put it down again and face the men.

"A few points to discuss today."

I'm filling in for Raiden, the club Pres. He's visiting his wife's family in Italy and taking his sweet ass time about it. They're all cooing over the new baby, and I guess the man deserves a vacation.

As Vice President, I'm keeping the club running in his absence. As his best friend, I'm keeping an eye on his daughter, Charlie.

I squeeze my hands together, thinking about Charlie out there with a bunch of drunk men. Davis will let me know if there's any trouble, but she's the type of girl who likes trouble.

"Let's keep this short."

I put my palms flat on the table and try not to think about Charlie.

First item on the agenda is a charity run for Women in Need that's on in a few months. A bunch of motorcycle clubs take part from all over the country. We ride in from our various corners of the country and meet up just outside of Colorado Springs for a weekend.

We usually support charities for veterans, but this year, with the opening of the women's refuge center, Lone Star brought this one to the table. His wife opened the center, and supporting Women in Need seems like a no-brainer to me.

But Judge has an issue.

"I support the charity of course, but it's the other clubs participating that I can't get behind."

I see his point. We're a legit motorcycle club, but not all MCs are.

"Do we really want to be associated with some of these other clubs?" Judge checks his notes. He's always got a notepad on him, which is probably why he's a kickass lawyer.

"The Underground Crows MC, riding in from the Sunset Coast. Their president served three years inside. Are these the type of clubs we want to be associated with?"

There are murmurs of assent from around the room.

"What did he go in for?" asks Arlo.

Next to Judge, Tech has his laptop open and is typing furiously. He frowns at the screen. "Illegal firearms."

"Ouch, that's bad." Arlo scratches his beard. "But these

guys, The Underground Crows, they're doing the charity run, so they can't be all bad."

"It could be a cover to move drugs." Judge folds his arms, and his mouth sets in a grim line. He's got zero tolerance for drugs. He's made up his mind about this club, and there'll be no persuading him otherwise.

"We're doing it for the charity," says Colter, otherwise known as Vintage due to his love of all things retro. "We don't have to associate with any other club we don't want to. We do our thing, and they do theirs."

"The charity is the important thing here," argues Lone Star from the screen of a laptop. "Let's not lose sight of that."

The men debate the issue for a few moments, going back and forth over the pros and cons of doing a charity run with clubs whose dealings aren't as legit as ours.

It's a debate we've had before. We're an MC, and not all MCs operate the way we do. The Wild Riders MC are ex-military men who love to ride. Some of us came here broken, some of us came here looking for somewhere to belong. I'm proud of what we've built up here, and our reputation matters, so I let the men debate and then I raise the gavel.

"Let's vote on it. All in favor of doing the Women in Need charity run, say aye."

There's a chorus of ayes around the room, and I count five raised hands including Lone Star's on the screen.

"Those against."

Judge raises his hand as does Badge, not surprising considering one's a lawyer and the other a sheriff. Tech raises his too, but I suspect it's because he'd rather stay indoors and play video games than do a ten day charity ride. Besides, he's got his two little ones to look after at home and no one to help.

"They ayes have it. We're doing the charity run." I slam the gavel down, and Judge huffs.

"No good will come of this," he mutters.

With the charity run sorted, I move onto the next piece of business.

"We've had an issue with the beer festival in Phoenix this weekend."

It's one of the biggest craft beer festivals on the circuit, and plenty of distributors attend looking for new products. It's a long way for us to go from North Carolina, but it could open up both the Midwest and the west coast markets for us.

Marcus and Hazel were supposed to take the pop-up peer truck to the festival. Since they hooked up, Hazel helps out at the bar sometimes, and her bubbly personality is great as a customer-facing person for the business. She's also a lot easier to look at than any of the hairy bikers in front of me.

We booked the festival months ago and they were going to do it together, with Hazel running the stall and Marcus meeting with distributors.

But since then, Hazel's gotten pregnant and has severe morning sickness. She's bedridden, doctor's orders, and Marcus won't leave her side.

"I need two volunteers to do the festival this weekend."

I scan the men in the room, but no one's volunteering.

"Arlo? Can you and Maggie go?" He's the most personable of us men. His road name is Prince, as in Prince Charming, and it's well deserved.

He shakes his head. "Sorry VP. We're visiting Maggie's folks this weekend. It's her dad's sixtieth birthday."

I can't ask him to miss such a family occasion. I run a hand down my face, wondering again if I should just cancel.

But Marcus has meetings set up with distributors, and it could expand our business nationwide.

"You know you're the best person for the job," Specs says as if reading my mind.

He sits quietly in the back of the room, his hands folded across whatever book this meeting disturbed him from. His glasses sit halfway down his nose.

"I can keep an eye on things for a few days."

I click my neck, thinking about it. He's right. I'm the best person to be in those meetings. The beer festival is just the backdrop for the business opportunities.

I nod curtly, making the decision. "I'll go. I can run the stall in between taking meetings. Specs will be in charge here."

Arlo presses his lips together and squints at me.

"What is it?" I bark.

"No offence, VP, but you're not exactly the right person to run the stall."

I glare at him. "What do you mean?"

He raises his eyebrows, and a smile tugs at his lips. "I mean, Barrels, you might need some backup on the stall."

The men suppress smiles, and I glower at them. But he has a point.

My road name is Barrels not only because I run a brewery, but because I was a staff sergeant in the military, and that makes me a no-nonsense man. I barrel through and get things done. I don't suffer fools, and it's why I stay out back in the brewery and not in the bar.

"Can anyone join me as the frontman for the stall?"

There are murmurs around the room about sick kids and absent wives. This place has turned into a kindergarten the last few years. You can't move without falling over someone's kid in the corridor. And they spend half the time in here, which means if one goes down with something they all do.

"All right, you pussies. Can anyone's old lady help us out? Colter. What about Danni?"

He sits up in his chair and shakes his head. "Kids have got the stomach bug. She had it too last night."

He coughs, and the men on either side of him lean away.

"What are you even doing here?" says Arlo. "We don't want it."

It was never this hard to get help before all the women came along.

"Is there anyone who isn't ill in this place?"

"How about Charlie?" Arlo suggests. "She'd be great at the festival. I bet she'd love it too."

An image of Charlie laughing with every hot-blooded male who wants a taste of beer passes through my mind.

"No way. She's needed here."

"I can spare her," says Travis. "I can't come with you, not with Kendra due so soon, but I can cover Charlie's shifts here."

I scowl at him. He's married to my little sister, which still makes my blood boil when I think about it too much. But I'm the only other family Kendra's got, and I don't want her to be alone while she's eight months pregnant.

That only leaves Charlie.

I promised Raiden I'd keep an eye on his daughter, and dragging her across the country to a craft beer festival where I'll be at meetings half the day and not able to ward off any unwanted male attention she gets doesn't feel like the protection I should give her.

But what other option is there?

"Fine," I say. "I'll go with Charlie. But the rest of you get yourselves better. We got a business to run."

There were never any tummy bugs in the military. In the military, we ran things with efficiency and no complaints. There were no sick babies or pregnant wives to work around.

I miss those days.

2

CHARLIE

"Cheers!"

The baby-faced Spiderman with a red cape hanging loose over one shoulder holds up his shot glass, and I clink it with mine.

The tequila burns on the way down and I follow it up with a slice of lemon, wincing at the bitterness on my tongue.

"Another one!" shouts Spiderman, but I shake my head.

"I got tables to clear."

One shot on the afternoon shift is enough for me. Besides, I don't want to encourage the drunk men at the bachelor party. There's a fine line between being friendly and being flirty.

A leotard clad arm shoots out and lands on my forearm.

"Have another, Caroline."

He's starting to slur, and I don't correct him that he

got my name wrong. Instead, I pointedly lift his hand off my arm.

"No, thank you."

My glance goes to the doorway, but Quentin isn't out of the meeting yet. If he saw one of these guys touching me, he'd flip.

He's been watching me like a hawk and he'll never admit it, but it's obvious Dad asked him to look out for me while he's away. And Quentin is a man who takes his duties seriously. Far too seriously.

I thought he was going to blow a gasket when I turned up in a short skirt the other day. Talk about an overreaction. He refused to let me work until I changed. Like I'm a sixteen-year-old going on a first date and not a twenty-two-year-old woman who can wear whatever the hell she wants.

I step away from the men at the bar and grab an empty drinks tray.

Davis raises his eyebrows at me.

"No more tequila."

I roll my eyes at him. "Are you telling me what to do now too?"

He chuckles. "I wouldn't dare, but Barrels will kick my ass if he knows I let you have that shot."

Davis is only a few years older than me, and nowhere near as intimidating as my father or his best friend, who still runs this place like he's the staff sergeant he was in the military.

"There are a lot of men around here who think they can tell me what to do."

A rebellious fire sparks inside me. Now Davis, who I consider a friend, is keeping an eye on me because Quentin asked him to, because Dad asked Quentin to. It makes me want to do something they'll all disapprove of just to get them to back off.

I spin around and head back to the other side of the bar.

Spiderman grins when I sidle up next to him.

"I will have another shot."

"That's my girl!" he crows. "Another round of shots, boys!"

There's a cheer from the group of men, and Davis scowls at me.

I smile at him sweetly, and his scowl deepens. I've just brought in another round of tequila shots, so I'm good for business.

At that moment Quentin strides in, and I try not to notice the way the hairs on the back of my neck bristle as his gaze scans the crowd and rests on me.

He holds my gaze for an intense beat. That one tequila shot must have affected me more than I know, because my breathing gets shallow and my pulse quickens.

Then he frowns and strides across the room, pushing between men until he reaches me.

"You okay?" He scans my face, and the concern in his eyes surprises me.

I give him a bright smile. "Just hanging out with the customers."

The scowl returns, and he glances at the men surrounding me.

"Not anymore. Your shift's finished."

My mouth drops open. He thinks I can't handle myself among a group of customers. But these men, while drunk, have been nothing but respectful.

"We were just about to get another round of tequila," Spiderman cuts in.

I wince, because it's the wrong thing to say.

Quentin fixes him with a steely staff sergeant stare. "No more shots."

Spiderman screws up his face and is about to complain when a less drunk friend pulls him back by the elbow. This man's dressed in a top hat and looks older than the others. Someone's older brother maybe, and the sensible one of the group.

He gives a curt nod to Quentin. "I'll get these guys out of your hair."

"I appreciate that."

Top hat pulls the men away from the bar, and I'm impressed that Quentin manages to clear a bachelor party just with his mere presence.

He's an imposing man, not as tall as some of the other guys here, but he's stocky. Thick shoulders and a body like a barrel, which is half the reason he got his road name, Barrels. It's also appropriate for the man who runs the brewery.

But I prefer to call him sergeant. With his tight-fitting khaki t-shirt, close cropped hair, and smoothly shaved chin, he looks like he never left the military. The rumor is he would have gone all the way to Sergeant Major if he'd stayed in. I can believe it with his permanent scowl and set ways.

Within moments the men are shuffling out the door, trailing pieces of fancy dress with them. All that's left are empty glasses and hardly touched food platters.

"How do you do that? Clear all the fun out of a bar so quickly?"

A ghost of a smile teases Quentin's lips. "Military training."

I start loading glasses onto a drinks tray, and Quentin helps with the clean-up.

"You don't need to work tonight, Charlotte."

He's the only person who calls me by my full name, and his deep rumbling voice sends a shiver down my spine. It's probably some military protocol thing.

I dump the last of the glasses on the bar where Davis is loading them into the dishwasher. "I'm fine. I'll get this cleared up and grab some food before the evening shift."

He shakes his head. "Travis is covering your shift."

I lean on the bar, wondering what this is all about. You can never be sure what's happening in this place. The club works together, and everyone generally has their assigned jobs in the restaurant, with the bike mechanics, or in the brewery. But if you're in the club, you're expected to help out where needed. I like that. It's like one big community.

"You're coming with me to the Phoenix Beer Festival."

I gape at him. "Are you serious?"

The festival's all the way across the country. Hazel and Marcus have been planning it for weeks.

"Hazel's sick, and Marcus won't leave her. Half my men have sick kids or wives. You and me are all there is."

"But…"

I want to protest just to be contrary, but it's been a while since I was on the open road, and I miss it. It will be nice to do something different for a few days even if it is with the uptight sergeant.

I shrug. "Okay."

He smiles, showing tiny crease lines by his eyes that give him a softer look.

"Good. Go home and pack your bags. We're going on a road trip."

3

QUENTIN

*M*y watch glows in the post dawn light. I told Charlie we were leaving at zero-six-hundred hours, and it's now zero-six-fourteen.

She's late.

I've been on the compound since zero-five hundred doing final checks of the truck and loading the last of the supplies. The mobile drinks truck is filled with bottles of our finest beer for the festival customer and samples of our best brews for potential new distributors.

I've got everything tied down and padded so we don't lose any bottles. My duffle bag is in the back, and I'm waiting with the door open to load Charlie's bag and hit the road.

I check my watch again. Zero-six-nineteen.

I grind my teeth together. We've got a lot of miles to cover in the next two days, and I like to start early.

The roar of a bike shatters the stillness of the morning, and Charlie comes into view. She's going too damn fast up the mountain road, and for a moment it looks like she's going to fly right past. She turns at the last moment, only slowing down enough to make the turn and not enough to avoid kicking up gravel in a skid.

Her bike tilts dangerously far to the left, and my heart leaps into my throat. Then she rights herself and pulls to a stop next to me, kicking up dust.

"God help me," I mutter under my breath.

This woman's going to give me a heart attack. Sometimes I think she's deliberately trying to provoke me.

She slides the helmet off her head, and a shock of pink hair tumbles out. It's mussed up and sticks up around her ears. Charlie gives a big yawn as she stretches, lifting her arms up in the air.

"Morning."

She isn't wearing her usual dark eyeliner and layers of makeup, and without the face armor she looks sleepy and adorable, like a kitten who's just woken up. But she's a kitten with claws, and I'm not fooled.

"You're late."

The softness of her expression immediately turns into a frown, and I regret my harsh tone.

"Not all of us are used to getting up at the ass-crack of dawn, sergeant."

Her hand runs through her hair, smoothing down the pixie cut as she gives a huge yawn.

"We got time to make a coffee?"

She slides off her bike and heads toward the back of the restaurant. The building is dark. No one's staying in the clubrooms at the moment, and Davis won't be here to open up for at least another few hours.

"Nope. We need to hit the road."

She stops and turns, and her hands go into her jacket pockets. She's all five-foot-four, puffed up and glowering at me like an angry cat.

"Where's your stuff?" I ask.

"In my saddle bags, why?"

I stare at her, trying to keep my voice calm. "To load it up so we can hit the road."

Realization dawns on her face. "We're not taking the bikes?"

"Of course we're not taking the bikes. We're going to a beer festival with the mobile bar." I fight to keep my voice calm. It's like she heard nothing of the briefing I gave her last night.

I think she's going to kick up a fuss, but Charlie just shrugs her shoulders.

"Okay. My stuff's in the saddle bag."

She strides back to her bike and hands me an over-sized purse. It doesn't look big enough for three nights away.

"This all you've got?"

She shrugs. "All I need is a toothbrush and spare underwear."

An image flashes through my head of Charlie's underwear. I bet it's black and lacy. I shake the thought out of my head, and grabbing her bag, launch it into the passenger seat.

"Get in. We're going."

She huffs at me, but there's an amused smile on her face. "You leaving your bike out here?"

"Hell no." I wouldn't leave my baby out in the elements for three days. "Colter will bring her into the workshop for me later. Leave your keys, and he'll do the same for you."

She strides across the parking lot and drops her keys into the slot by the door to the workshop. Her black leather pants hug her curvy ass and make my palms sweat. I hope she brought something else to wear at the festival or every hot-blooded man in the county will be hanging around her.

The thought makes my blood boil. I make a mental note to stop by a clothing shop and get her a sensible blouse and long skirt to wear. Something baggy. Then I dismiss the idea. The day Charlie lets me dress her in sensible clothes with be the day hell freezes over.

I climb into the driver's seat and watch her stride across the parking lot toward me.

This is going to be a hell of a few days.

4
CHARLIE

Quentin glares at me from the inside of the truck, and just to make him wait, I take my sweet-ass time walking across the parking lot.

On the way past my bike, I check the saddle bags and redo one of the straps to make it tighter. When I reach the van, Quentin is drumming his fingers on the steering wheel and looks about ready to blow a gasket.

I'm not sure why I love getting under his skin so much, but I do. There's something about his rigid ways that make me want to push all his buttons. The guy needs to relax and stop taking life so seriously.

The engine's already running when I slide into the passenger seat. He's in his usual tight khaki t-shirt, and his leather MC jacket is draped in the space between us.

Before I can get my belt on the van jerks forward, and I almost go flying out of my seat.

"Hey, watch it."

I glare at Quentin, but he's looking straight ahead.

There's a hint of a smile on his lips, and if I didn't know him as my father's serious friend who never jokes around, I'd say he did that on purpose.

I click my belt in as we pull out of the lot and onto the mountain road. I'm about to say something snarky when my gaze fixes on two takeout coffee mugs in the cupholders hanging off the dash. There's steam coming out of the top of them.

"You made us coffee?"

"It's probably cold by now," he mutters.

I take the cup closest to me and take a sip. It's super sweet with no milk, exactly how I like it. How the hell does Quentin know how I take my coffee?

He must have been here super early to get into the clubhouse, start the machine, and make us coffees to take with us.

Maybe the man's not such a hard-ass after all.

"Thank you."

He pulls a piece of folded paper out of his pocket and shoves it at me.

"What's this?" I take the paper and unfold it with one hand.

"Our itinerary. I've got it memorized, but I printed you a copy."

An itinerary. Of course it is. Quentin's probably even got bathroom stops planned out on here.

"We've got sixteen hundred and forty-four miles to cover, and we're already..." He checks his watch. "Thirty-two minutes late."

I stare at him. "Thirty-two minutes, really? You couldn't just say thirty?"

He gives me a look as if I'm the crazy one.

I fold the itinerary up without looking at it and stuff it in my purse. I pull out my makeup bag and flip down the visor to get to the mirror underneath.

Wide eyes stare back at me and skin too smooth to be an adult's. I hate how I look without makeup. Vulnerable and young and like a little girl pretending to be a grown-up.

I grab my tube of concealer and get to work. First I smooth over the freckles on my nose, and then I apply a layer of foundation.

I take out my eyeliner and lean forward. The van bumps over the mountain road, and if I'm not careful I'll take my eye out.

I put my foot up on the dashboard and rest my elbow against it for stability.

"No boots on the dash."

I turn to look at Quentin with my eyeliner poised in my hand and keep my foot on the dash.

"Then you'll have to pull over while I do this, because there's no way to keep my hand steady, and I don't want to poke my eye out."

He frowns at me. "I'm not stopping so you can do your makeup."

Of course he's not. It wasn't on the itinerary.

"Fine then."

I keep my foot on the dash and lean forward. As I get close to my eye, the van swerves.

"Hey!" I glance over, and Quentin's staring straight ahead at the road. "Did you do that on purpose?"

He keeps looking straight ahead. "I don't know what you mean, Charlotte. But you need to get your boots off my dash."

Dawn is breaking over the mountain ranges and his profile is backlit, showing off his strong jawline and pronounced forehead. His hair is cropped short, and if there's any grey it's hidden in the blonde. The outline of his muscles can be seen through his tight t-shirt. It's obvious Quentin still works out. He might have left the military, but it's never left him.

His tone is calm and sure, and when he says my name a shiver dances down my spine. He's used to commanding men, and he's good at it.

Slowly, I remove my boot from the dash. A ghost of a smile appears across Quentin's face and that tugs at all the rebelliousness inside me. I can't let him win a total victory.

I undo the laces of my black steel capped boots and slide them off. My foot comes up on the dash, and Quentin glares at my bright pink fluffy socks.

"You said no boots."

He looks away, muttering under his breath. I lean forward with my eyeliner, smiling to myself as I finish my make up.

"You don't need all that makeup anyway," he says.

I bat my eyes at him "Are you calling me beautiful?"

He looks away, embarrassed, and I laugh. "I'm just fucking with ya."

"And don't cuss. It doesn't sound nice to hear you cuss."

"So men are allowed to swear and woman aren't? Hello, we're living in the twenty-first century. I will not be beholden to some male ideal of what a woman is meant to be."

He rolls his eyes. "Jeez, Charlie. It doesn't sound nice for anyone to cuss. I heard enough of it in the military, and I don't like hearing it now. There are better words to use to describe something. You've got a brain in your head. Use it."

I stare at him. I never knew he had so many ideas about what's proper and what's not. There's more to my father's best friend than an uptight ex-army sergeant.

"I'm just messing with ya."

He nods curtly. "See, there's no need to swear."

"No fucking need," I say under my breath.

Quentin gives me a sharp look. I hide my smile behind my hand, and he shakes his head and looks back to the road.

I'm travelling with the world's biggest grump. This is going to be one long road trip.

5
QUENTIN

I pull the truck into a parking space and kill the engine. Charlie unclips her seat belt and stretches.

"Where are we?"

We've parked in front of the town square of a bustling small town. A woman pushes a stroller past the truck and takes a seat on a park bench near a box of bright flowers. People mill about, walking briskly or sitting in groups on concrete stairs that surround the centerpiece of the town square.

Charlie peers out the window, and her head tilts up to take in the statue at the center of the square. It's an eagle made of brass panels and it stands as tall as two tanks. The wings are outstretched, encompassing the town square. It would look impressive if it wasn't for the giant clock embedded in its chest. The proud bird has been turned into a time piece.

"Kings County, Tennessee."

She wrinkles her nose. "Never heard of it. Is this where the festival is?"

She hasn't read her itinerary. "We won't reach the festival until tomorrow night. This is our lunch stop."

Charlie frowns. "But we've been driving for hours."

The eagle clock shows it's just after midday.

"We've been driving for five and a half hours."

She slides her feet into her boots and goes to rest the left foot on the dash to tie the laces. I give her a pointed look, and the foot hovers in the air before coming down on the seat instead.

It's a small victory, but I'll take it. She's not defying me on everything.

While Charlie gets her boots laced, I slide out of the cab. It gives me an opportunity to stretch out my back where she can't see. It's been aching for the last hundred miles, but I won't let Charlie see that.

I do some stretches, and when I hear her door slam, I straighten up and walk around to the front of the truck.

"Was this place on the itinerary?"

Charlie smirks at me as if forward planning is something to be ashamed of. If it was left to her, she'd wing the entire trip.

"A lunch stop is on the itinerary. I chose this town because of the famous eagle clock."

Charlie glances up at the weird clock tower. "Really?"

"No. I randomly took an off ramp and here we are. The eagle is a happy accident."

Her mouth falls open in mock surprise. "Did you just make a joke?"

27

I give her a deadpan look. "I never joke."

I can't help the smile that tugs at my lips, and when Charlie sees it, she smiles too. I don't usually joke, but I like making Charlie smile.

"Let's walk. We need to stretch our legs."

The town square borders a river, and we walk along the path for a ways. Swans glide across the water, and a small mechanical boat cruises next to them. Across the lake, a man crouches next to a small boy, helping him use the remote control that controls the boat. The boy smiles with delight, and the man ruffles his hair.

There's a pang in my chest as I watch them. I dedicated my life to the military, and there wasn't room for anyone else. It's a tough life on families, and I never regretted my decision.

But the last few years, seeing all my MC brothers settle down with kids, I wonder if there's something I'm missing.

"Ooh donuts!"

Charlie pulls me out of my thoughts, and when I turn she's got a huge grin on her face. The sun catches on the pink highlights of her hair, and her eyes light up in delight.

She practically skips over to the donut van that's parked near the lake.

"Dana's Donut Delights" is written in cursive script on the top of the van, and a woman who looks not much older than Charlie loads a tray of colorful donuts into the display cabinet. They're decorated in thick pink frosting with chocolate sprinkles.

Not what I'd consider lunch food, but Charlie's already talking with the woman. When she turns to put the tray behind her, I notice her belly is round with a baby bump and her cheeks are rosy. Darn fertile woman everywhere I go. I wonder what Charlie would look like with a pregnant belly; her cheeks flushed like this woman's.

The thought stops me in my tracks. Why the hell am I imagining Charlie pregnant?

"Quentin?"

Charlie's looking at me with concern in her eyes, and I realize she's said something and I have no idea what it is.

"You okay? You look like you've seen a ghost."

I shake the image out of my head and swallow hard.

"We're not having donuts for lunch," I say a little too harshly, and hate myself for it when the smile slips from Charlie's face.

She narrows her eyes at me and turns back to the woman.

"Two of the pink ones please."

Two minutes later, I'm sitting on a park bench taking a bite out of a pink donut. As soon as my lips close around it, the sweet taste of chocolate and sugar frosting and dough floods my mouth.

Charlie moans, and when I look over her eyes are closed as she chews slowly. She moans again, and there's a twinge in my groin at the sound.

I stand up quickly, and her eyes fly open.

"This is good, right?" She's got a sparkle in her eye that lights up her entire face. I turn around so she won't see the effect her moans are having on me.

"It's a good donut," I concede. "But I need something else."

I set off back down the way we came to the main square. Charlie follows, still munching on her donut. I can't risk looking at her or this twinge in my loins is going to turn into something more.

She just needs to finish the donut and stop looking so sexy while she does it.

"I'll have yours if you don't want it."

"No." I clasp the paper bag with the remains of my donut close to my chest. The last thing I need is for Charlie to moan over another donut.

"I'm saving it for dessert."

She chuckles at me. "I didn't know you had a sweet tooth."

And I didn't know you looked so damn sexy when you eat.

"There's a sandwich shop." I cross the town square, choosing the least sexy food I can find. No one's going to moan over an egg sandwich.

A few minutes later, we're on the steps under the eagle clock munching on egg and cress sandwiches. There's no moaning, no pregnant woman, and I'm able to think straight and look Charlie in the eye.

"What made you leave the military?" she asks.

I finish my mouthful, getting my thoughts together. I don't talk about this much, but then again, no one ever asks.

"My parents passed."

Charlie places a hand on my arm, and the warmth of her touch is comforting. "I'm so sorry. That's terrible."

"It was a long time ago, and I've come to terms with it." I still miss them of course, but I've learned to live with it. "I thought I would be in the military for life, but after they passed, Kendra went off the rails. I was the only family she had, so I came home."

Charlie drops her hand from my arm. "I heard Kendra was wild until she settled down with Travis."

I grunt at the comment, because I've still not come to terms with my oldest friend hooking up with my little sister. Even though they're married now and expecting their first baby.

"Not as wild as you."

Charlie cocks her head, and a smile plays on her lips. "I'm not as wild as my dad thinks I am."

It's my turn to be surprised. "So you didn't ride across the country on your own to get to his wedding?"

Charlie shrugs. "Oh yeah, I did that."

I shake my head. Raiden was happy when his daughter turned up for his wedding but furious when he found out how she got here. A three day road trip on her own. All the way from California biking alone on the roads and staying in cheap roadside motels.

"I'm independent. I'll claim that. But I'm not wild."

31

"Careless is what that is. A woman riding on her own."

She sticks her chin out, and her eyes flash dangerously. "You think because I'm a woman I shouldn't do things on my own?"

"I think there are a lot of assholes out there who could do you harm."

"Perhaps." She pokes at the egg in her sandwich. "I think there's a lot of fear out there. And I refuse to put restrictions on myself because there may be a bad man lurking."

Anything could have happened to Charlie on the roads. Her bike could have gotten a flat, she might have had an accident. It's not just the fact that she's a woman biking alone. Long distance riding alone is dangerous for anyone.

"Anything could have happened."

"But it didn't."

I run my hand through my hair in exasperation. She's lucky nothing happened.

"Why did you decide to stay anyway? Why not go back to Santa Cruz?"

Charlie takes a bite of sandwich and takes her time chewing before answering. "Dad wasn't around much when I was growing up," she says quietly.

It's true. The military life is hard on families, and in the early days we were deployed for long stretches in Iraq. It put huge pressure on his new family.

Raiden and I were in the same platoon. Both

sergeants working up the ranks, we became good friends.

I remember the day he got the call from his ex-wife, Charlie's mom, telling him she was moving back to California with Charlie. Raiden was devastated, but there's not a lot you can do from a war zone.

By the time he got out of the military, Charlie was sixteen and making her own choices.

"It's nice to get to know him again," she says quietly. "It's different here than California."

She looks like she wants to say more and I wait, but she crumples the empty sandwich wrapper and stands up.

"Is there somewhere to get a coffee for the road?"

The smile is back that doesn't quite meet her eyes, and I wonder what haunts her from California.

I'm only her father's friend, the bossy ex-sergeant who disapproves of her choices. Only I don't disapprove. The more time I spend with Charlie, I approve of her very much.

6

QUENTIN

*M*y lower back aches from too long in the driver's seat. I'm used to the freedom of a bike, and sitting up here is torture. If it wasn't for Charlie beside me, I'd probably give it up and drive home.

She offered to drive, but after an hour of her breaking every speed limit, I took the wheel back.

She put her headphones in sometime after dinner. We couldn't agree on music we both liked. And sometime past the Oklahoma state line, she fell asleep.

Her pink socked foot found its way onto the dashboard again, and she sleeps with her leg propped up and her head back.

The radio plays softy in the background, a local station pumping out hits from the nineties, which Charlie calls old man music. How anyone can think Foo Fighters and Green Day are old man music is beyond me. It's the music I grew up with, and I sing along quietly to a Blink-182 classic while Charlie dozes.

We stopped a few hours ago for dinner, but I wanted to put some more miles behind us before turning in for the night.

There's no hotel booked on the itinerary for tonight. Marcus and Hazel figured they'd find a place along the highway wherever they wanted to stop. We're just out of Amarillo when I pull into a brightly lit motel.

The neon lights flash in the darkness as I bring the truck to a stop.

Charlie doesn't stir. Her lips are parted slightly, and a strand of hair falls over her cheeks. With her eyes closed she seems softer, vulnerable.

Her hair falls over her face, shielding her eyes, and I hook a pink strand behind my finger and tuck it behind her ear.

Charlie stirs, and her eyes flicker open. Her breath catches when she finds me leaning over her. Up this close, I notice the dappled green of her eyes in the neon flash of the hotel lights. They look like a stormy ocean.

She smiles softly at me. "Are we there?"

Her breath grazes my lips, and a jolt of heat races through my body. I jerk back to my side of the truck and push the door open.

"Not even close But I need a few hours sleep."

My heart races as I slam the door shut behind me. My thoughts are in turmoil over the pretty woman in the cab of the truck. She was so close I could have kissed her. I almost did. And that would be madness.

For one mad moment, I got caught up in her beauty, in her youthful skin and sleepy face. She must have been terrified to wake up and find an old man like me ogling her.

I shake my head at my folly. To think a young woman with all her life ahead of her, a woman with an independent spirit, would want to kiss an old army sergeant like me.

As I walk to the reception desk, the cool air of the night calms my racing heart and brings me to my senses.

I secure two rooms next to each other, and by the time I head back to the truck my heart is beating normally, and all thoughts of kissing Charlie are out of my head.

Until I see her striding over to the Coke machine. She's pulled her boots back on, and in her tight leathers every curve of her body sways as she walks, from her full hips to her round butt and the confident set of her shoulders.

My mouth goes dry, and my heart rate leaps up again. I stop in my tracks just to watch her strut across the parking lot.

I'm not the only one watching.

A low wolf whistle pierces the night. My head snaps around to the rusty pickup parked across from our truck. Two men sit in the front seat smoking. Judging from the sweet aroma floating across the parking lot, it's not a cigarette they're passing to each other.

Charlie ignores the whistle and keeps striding to the Coke machine. But her shoulders sag a little, like they've snatched a bit of her confidence away.

My fists clench, and I stride over to the pickup. They

don't see me, too intent on watching Charlie. One of the men whistles again and calls out to her.

This time Charlie flicks them the bird without looking around.

"Fuck off," she calls over her shoulder.

The men laugh, and that irritates me even more. The one in the passenger seat cups his hands around his mouth and cat calls.

He's so focused on Charlie, or so stoned, that he doesn't see me approaching. I wait until I'm standing right by his window before leaning in.

"Boo!"

The man screams. He jumps in his seat, and the joint falls out of his fingers and lands on his lap.

"What the fuck!"

His legs jerk, and smokes rises from his crotch as he pats at it frantically.

I remain staring at him, enjoying watching the damage he's doing to himself.

"Didn't anyone ever teach you not to disrespect a woman?"

I stride around the front of the car, and the man in the driver's seat stares at me through the windshield. His eyes are bloodshot and wide with fear.

"S-Sorry. We didn't know she was with you, man."

He fumbles with the ignition and drops his keys. They fall between the seat and the door and he reaches for them with one hand, not wanting to take his eyes off me.

"I'm not with him." Charlie strides across the parking lot with a look of thunder on her face.

The guy lets out a terrified squeak when he sees Charlie stalking towards him. Pride surges in me at her confident stride.

"What the fuck is the matter with you? Just because a woman walks across a parking lot you think you have the right to harass her?"

Sweat beads on the man's forehead as he searches for his keys. His buddy has retrieved the joint, and he pats his smoldering crotch.

"Go man, just go!" he screams.

"I'm trying," whimpers the driver.

He finds his keys, but he's shaking so much he can't get the key in the ignition. Now it's not me he's staring at but Charlie, stalking across the parking lot like an avenging angel.

"Learn some respect, dipshit."

She reaches him just as he finally gets the key in the ignition and the truck roars to life. But he's too late. Charlie reaches through the window and pours Coke all over his crotch.

The man jerks the pickup forward, and Charlie pulls her arm out of the way just in time. The tires spin as the men take off.

They pull out with a screech and weave onto the road.

"I told you there were assholes around," I mutter.

"And I told you I can look after myself."

Charlie watches them go with her arm outstretched,

the can dripping soda onto the tarmac. Her breathing is heavy, and when she turns to me her eyes sparkle with mirth.

"You think we scared them good enough?" She laughs a deep throaty laugh. Her entire face lights up, and the heaviness of the situation dissipates.

"You should have seen their faces," I chuckle. "They were more terrified of you than me."

The absurdity of the situation hits me. I'm an ex-military first class sergeant wearing an MC patch. But Charlie striding across the tarmac scared them more.

Laughter rolls through me. "Your face...I thought you were going to hit him."

She doubles up in laughter and grabs my shoulder. "You should have seen his face when he saw you standing at the window."

She does a mock terrified high-pitched screech, and we both crack up.

I'm still chuckling as I take the bags up the concrete stairs. I hand Charlie the key to her room, and as she takes it her fingers brush mine. A shock of energy races up my fingers and surges through my body.

My gaze darts to hers and she's looking at me intently, the laugher gone from her eyes. She must have felt the spark too.

"Thank you for sticking up for me." Her breath caresses my cheeks, and I catch a scent of the apple pie she had at dinner.

"I'll always stick up for you."

Her hand drops with the key, but she doesn't go into

her room. If I was going to kiss her, now would be the moment. When we're so close and sore from laughing and my heart's battering against my ribcage like machine gun fire.

I lean forward and she parts her lips, ready for me.

Then reality crashes into my brain. She's the Pres's daughter. She's fifteen years younger than me. We're soaring from the adrenaline of the encounter, that's all this is.

"Goodnight, Charlotte." I kiss her on the cheek and step away before I do something that will end badly for both of us.

Disappointment flickers across her face, and she glances down.

"Goodnight, Quentin."

I wait until she's in her room with the door locked behind her before going into mine. I shut the door behind me and lean against it, breathing hard.

Knowing there's only a wall separating us, I sleep fretfully. Tossing and turning and wondering what would have happened if I'd followed my instincts and kissed her apple pie lips.

A whole lot of trouble is what would have happened.

Charlie is wild, she's Raiden's daughter, and I have no right thinking indecent thoughts about her.

But it's indecent thoughts that invade my dreams all night.

7

CHARLIE

I wake to the sound of vehicles rumbling down the highway. When I pull my curtains back, I'm greeted with the grey of the parking lot and the super cheerful hotel sign, lights still flashing hopefully in the daytime.

Despite the traffic noise and lumpy hotel bed, I slept like a log. I went to sleep dreaming of the big ex-sergeant next door and wondering what his lips would taste like.

We were so close last night I thought he was going to kiss me. But I must have been imagining it. After weeks of trying to break down Quentin's armor, I've come to realize he won't cave.

It's obvious he desires me, but he's bought into the lie that society has been telling him. That I'm too young or something.

Whatever his reasons, he's holding onto them.

I take a long hot shower with my music going, singing along to Boygenius.

When I turn the shower off, there's a furious thumping on the door. I wrap the threadbare towel around me as best I can. My boobs are barely covered and one thigh sticks out. These towels aren't made for curvy girls like me.

"Are you awake in there?"

Quentin thumps on the door, and I pull it open a crack. His face is lined, and there are dark circles under his eyes.

"You look like you haven't slept."

He waves a piece of paper at me, and it's that damned itinerary he's so fond of.

"We're meant to be on the road."

I open the door further, and the words die on his lips as his gaze slides down my body. The way I'm clasping the towel together pushes my breasts up, and water glistens on my skin.

I should shut the door and get myself decent, but I like the look Quentin's giving me. My skin heats under his gaze, and I arch my back slightly to push my breasts out even further.

His gaze skims my thighs where the towel barely contains all of my body, and he swallows hard. His mouth opens, but nothing comes out.

The uptight ex-army sergeant is lost for words, and it's all because I'm dripping wet in a towel.

I wonder what he'd do if I let the towel drop. If I let go of the one corner under my left armpit where I'm holding it up and let it pool on the floor.

Would he take me like I'm aching for him to do?

Would his muscular arms wrap around me? Would he carry me to the bed, or would he push me up against the wall while I wrapped my thighs around him?

My pulse quickens, and my heart's hammering so hard in my chest that he must hear it. My fingers twitch, about to relinquish the towel.

"Hey asshole, you done knocking? Some of us are trying to sleep."

A man in loose pajamas appears on the walkway behind Quentin, and instead of dropping the towel I tighten my grip on it.

I take a step back into my room, not wanting the stranger to see me half naked.

"We leave in five minutes."

Quentin's scowl is back, and he closes my door as he turns to the man.

I lean against the door, listening to the muffled voices. Quentin gives the guy a dressing down, but I don't hear what's said. My heart's beating too fiercely.

I almost dropped the towel. I almost exposed myself to Quentin to see what would happen.

There's an ache between my legs, and I slide my hand down my body. My skin is slick with water, and my nipples are hard. My hand continues between my legs, and I moan softly when I press against my sensitive nub.

Would Quentin be rough with me or gentle? I can never tell what side of him I'm going to get.

I imagine his angry energy throwing me onto the bed, his arms pinning me down as I writhe underneath him.

My movements become faster, and I'm panting hard.

43

I imagine him kissing me roughly as he grinds into me, thrusting into me and showing no mercy.

The pressure builds as I imagine him shoving me onto my knees and taking me roughly from behind, the headboard banging against the cheap hotel wall sending particleboard flying. I imagine him working my clit with his capable fingers as he loses control in me.

The orgasm races through my body, and I bite my cheek to stop from crying out. My fingers are soaked and my pussy throbs and I rub myself again, teasing out another climax. My eyes are shut tight, keeping me in the fantasy of Quentin pounding me over and over again as he loses control. Touching me and caressing me and taking everything he needs from me until we both come again and again.

I'm shaking from my third orgasm when there's a bang on the door. My eyes fly open, and I scramble up from where I sunk to the floor.

"Two minutes and I'm leaving."

I pant hard at the sound of his voice. He's gruff and commanding and a pain in the ass, but no man has ever invaded my thoughts the way he does. I've never done what I just did while thinking about a man.

I should feel satisfied, but the dull ache between my legs is worse than before. I've fantasized about Quentin, and it's made me hungry for the real thing.

8

QUENTIN

*T*en minutes later Charlie's door finally opens, and she emerges onto the walkway fully made up and in her black leathers with a smile on her face. She waves at me, leaning against the side of the truck as if she's not got a care in the world.

I check my watch pointedly. It's zero-seven-thirty-six. Thirty six minutes after the time I wanted to hit the road. And an hour and thirty six minutes later than what's on the itinerary.

I made allowances for her yesterday and drove as late as I could so she could have an hour to sleep in this morning. She's obviously not used to getting up at six. Or at seven, it turns out.

But as Charlie comes down the stairs with a smile just for me, it's hard to stay cross at her.

"Is there time for breakfast?"

I scoff, because she really has no idea how to keep to a schedule.

"Breakfast was an hour ago."

She frowns, and she can be pissed with me. That's fine just as long as she gets in the van and we get on the road. There are still a lot of miles to cover today.

A man walks past with a large German shepherd, and Charlie smiles and walks over to them both.

"Hello big guy."

She coos at the dog who looks like it would take her head off. But the big hound sticks his chin out to be tickled, and when Charlie crouches down next to him he licks her face.

"I love dogs."

She speaks to the dog and owner for a few moments, and I watch them with my arms folded.

Ever since I saw Charlie with only a towel wrapped around her this morning, I've had an uncomfortable ache in my loins.

It's been a long time since I was with a woman, and it's a painful irony that the first one who makes my dick stir is Charlie.

It's impossible to act on my attraction to her. But when she opened her door dripping wet in a towel, it was hard to remember the reasons why. The image is burnt into my retinas. I would have gone back to my room to relieve myself, but I'd already turned in the key.

Instead I took a walk along the highway and got us some breakfast. I knew she wouldn't be down in five minutes, and I was correct.

I'd only just managed to cool my overheated blood

when she appeared looking sassy as fuck in her tight leather outfit and with her war paint on.

I'm not the only one who's noticed.

The young man with the dog is blatantly staring at her tits while she's patting his dog.

Jealousy flares inside of me. I stalk over to them and lay a hand on Charlie's shoulder, pulling her up and pulling her tits out of the man's line of sight.

"Time to go."

The dog growls at me, and Charlie scowls and shrugs her arm out of my grip.

"You're so upright."

She heads over to the truck and I follow, turning back once to make sure the man isn't watching her ass.

That's my ass to look at.

The thought slides through my brain even though I know it's absurd. Charlie isn't mine; she never will be. But damned if I'm going to let every man ogle her.

"Are you always so grumpy in the mornings?" Charlie asks as she slides into the truck.

"Yes," I mutter.

She opens her mouth to say something then shuts it again when she sees the steaming coffee in the cupholder and the paper bag on her side of the dash.

She opens the bag and finds the bacon and cheese croissant I got for her.

"You bought me breakfast?"

Her voice is incredulous, and the smile she turns on me is so bright I have to look away.

I put the van in reverse and back out of the parking spot, then swing her around and head onto the highway.

"I don't want you complaining about being hungry all morning," I mutter.

But that's not why I bought her breakfast.

I bought her breakfast because I know she loves bacon croissants and a black coffee in the morning.

Because it's the little things that make Charlie smile, and I want to see her smile when she bites into that greasy croissant.

Charlie leans over and ruffles my hair.

"You may be an uptight grump, but you're the most thoughtful uptight grump I know."

I keep my eyes on the road and the scowl on my face, but inside my heart melts a little. My chest feels light, and the entire world looks a little bit brighter.

9

CHARLIE

"*A*nimal, vegetable, or mineral?" Quentin asks for the hundredth time.

I cast around the landscape, trying to think of an object that I haven't already come up with. We've been playing this game across most of New Mexico right after we ran out of ideas for I Spy. There's not a lot to spy when you're driving through the plains of New Mexico.

My gaze wanders back to Quentin. His profile is more relaxed than I've seen him. A light stubble coats his chin, a sign that the afternoon's getting late, and there's a hint of a smile on his usually serious features.

He glances over at me with his eyebrows raised. "Well? We haven't got all day."

We both laugh at what's become a running joke. The day has stretched before us, and we've spent it playing silly car games and taking it in turns to choose the music.

I don't mind his alt rock too much, and he's tapped along respectfully to Boygenius and Mitski.

In twenty years of music, the sentiment hasn't changed. The songs are about lost love, feeling like an outsider, and trying to find your place in life. Universal themes no matter the decade of music.

"Animal," I say.

"Kangaroo," Quentin says immediately, making me chuckle. There are no kangaroos out here.

"No."

"Is it a mammal?"

"Yes."

"Is it domesticated?"

I give Quentin an assessing look. "Maybe?"

He glances at me and frowns. "What do you mean maybe? Either it's been domesticated or not."

I hide my laugher behind my hands. He doesn't know that he's the animal I've chosen.

"Okay, yes. It's domesticated."

He thinks for a moment, causing little frown lines to appear on his forehead. I like the way he frowns when he's thinking, like everything he does is of importance, even a guessing game.

"Does it sleep in a barn?"

I can't stop laughing now, thinking about Quentin sleeping in a barn.

"No."

"Is it a dog?"

"No."

His frown deepens. "Does it sleep on its owner's bed?"

Imagining Quentin curled up at the end of my bed makes me laugh so hard I double over.

"Maybe. I mean it could."

He eyes me suspiciously. "What's so funny?"

I wipe the tears from my eyes and check my makeup in the mirror. My finger wipes up a smudge of mascara.

"Does it have fur?"

This elicits another round of laughter. "I'm not sure. It might be hairy."

"Hmmm." He gives me the side eye as suspicion dawns on him.

"It's me, isn't it?"

I'm laughing so hard I can barely speak. I just nod my head. Then Quentin's laughing too, a deep belly laugh that rumbles out of his throat and sets me off even more.

He laughs with an abandon that I don't usually see in the ex-military sergeant.

It's nice. It's a different side to him, and I suddenly wonder what he'd be like as a life partner. What would it be like to have this tough man by my side, making him belly laugh whenever I could?

The tough man with the soft side that only I seem to bring out in him.

The thought sobers me up. I've never had a relationship before, not a real one. The boys I ran around with in California were just that. Boys. They were always too intimidated by me, too scared to contradict me, and too in awe of my tits.

Not Quentin. He has no problem telling me when I've gone too far. He has standards, and I like that. The only problem is those same standards might stop him from doing exactly what he wants with me.

"Let's put some music on."

I choose my Pink playlist and turn up the volume. As the landscape rushes by, I think about how nice it would be to have someone to laugh with every day.

QUENTIN

$\mathcal{W}$e make good time, and it's just past 6 p.m. when we pull into the small town on the outskirts of Phoenix that's hosting the beer festival. Hazel booked a hotel, and it's a cute old style county inn with a pub and restaurant and some rooms up top.

I grab the clear folder with the itinerary and booking details and head into reception.

Charlie follows me out of the truck, stretching and yawning and blinking in the evening light.

The woman at the reception counter is middle-aged and greets us with a warm smile.

"I'm Sharon," she says. "Welcome to the Red Goose Inn."

I check the itinerary for the booking number and rattle it off.

"You here for the beer festival?" she asks.

I tell her about our stall at the festival, and we

exchange pleasantries. It's a family run inn, and her husband Vinny turns up as she hands over the keys.

"Come down for dinner when you're ready," Sharon says. "We've got live music tonight. My daughter Dina's singing." She says it proudly, and I smile and promise to stop by to hear her daughter.

She hands over an old-fashioned brass key.

"Room twelve. Straight up the stairs and to the left."

I stare at the key, waiting for her to give us another one, but she smiles as if that's it.

"We should have two rooms."

The moment I say it, I realize my mistake. Hazel booked the accommodation for her and Marcus. Of course she would have booked only one room.

The woman taps her computer and frowns. "I've only got a booking for one double room."

Charlie leans on the counter next to me, and I can tell without even looking at her that she's laughing. Darn woman finds everything funny. But this is serious. I cannot share a room with Charlie.

"Is there another room available?"

The woman shakes her head. "I'm afraid not. We're all booked for the festival. The entire town will be."

She looks generally concerned, and I don't want to make her feel bad, but this is bad. I run a hand through my hair and turn to Charlie.

"Looks like you're stuck with me, sergeant."

Thoughts of sleeping in the same bed as Charlie flood my brain. Her body entwined with mine, her hot breath on my skin...

"Is there a twin room we can swap with?"

At least separate beds would be something.

The woman shakes her head, and her look of sympathy makes me feel like an ass for making such a fuss. "I'm afraid not. The only twin is taken by a pair of elderly sisters, and I'm reluctant to move them."

"Of course."

Charlie snatches the key out of my hand. "Come on, sergeant. I promise not to steal your virtue in the night."

But the twinkle in her eye tells me she finds this amusing.

Charlie grabs her bag and heads up the stairs. I watch her go, and my eyes are drawn to her incredibly tight pants and perfect round ass.

My dick stirs to attention, and I swallow hard.

"Will it be a problem?" the woman asks, concerned at our predicament.

Yeah, it will be a big problem. A big hard-on sized problem. But the woman's been nothing but kind, and I don't want to make her feel bad. Besides, what other choice is there?

"No, it's fine. Thank you, we'll come down soon for dinner."

She looks relieved, and I give her a curt nod before following Charlie up the stairs to our room.

I don't know how I'm going to survive two nights in the same room with Charlie without doing something we'll both regret.

11

CHARLIE

The woman's voice soars over the rumble of diners chatting and pierces my very soul.

She sings about loss and heartache, and I feel it right in my bones. She plays a baby grand piano that sits on a raised stage in the corner of the inn's dining room.

Standing next to the stage with crossed arms is a gruff-looking man whose scowl could rival Quentin's. He watches the crowd with his beady eyes as if she's a famous songstress at a stadium concert and not playing to a dinner crowd of thirty in a cozy inn.

The song finishes and I applaud loudly and put my fingers in my mouth and whistle. The woman looks my way and smiles. As she turns I glimpse a scar on her right cheek, the side she kept hidden from the audience. It only ads to her mystic, the beautiful singer in the small inn on the edge of town. It makes me wonder what her story is.

"She's fantastic."

Quentin sits next to me at a small round table. Not wanting to have his back to the singer, he shuffled his chair around so that he's next to me. The occasional brush of our thighs under the table sends a zing of energy up my body.

"She's all right," he mutters.

Quentin's still grumpy about having to share a room and a bed with me. But there's nothing we can do about it, so why worry?

I find the thought of sleeping next to the man thrilling. Maybe it's the universe giving us the push we need to get close to each other.

I take a bite of my grilled chicken and watch the woman on stage. She stands up, and two small children run out from a booth in the corner and climb on stage with her.

She crouches down despite her sequenced dress and takes one of them into her arms. The smile she turns on the child is infectious. The other child is scooped up by the rough-looking man, and his expression softens.

There's a pang in my heart as I watch the family together.

"I'll be back after this break," the woman says into the mic.

Vinny gets on stage. He owns the inn with his wife who we met at reception. He's skinny with shoulder length black hair and wears a black leather jacket.

"Show your appreciation for Dina." His voice is husky, like a man who's smoked his entire life.

There's another round of applause, and the woman,

Dina, smiles graciously before leaving the platform with her family. They scoot into a booth, and the woman changes from sexy songstress to doting mother.

Vinny brings them a plate of chips and salad, and the kids dive in eagerly.

"Do you want kids?"

My attention snaps back to Quentin, his question catching me off guard.

I never thought I wanted kids. My childhood wasn't the happiest, moving from place to place. Dad was away with the military, and when mom left him and took me to Santa Cruz in California, she spent more time getting stoned than being a doting mother. We moved from town to town but kept coming back to Santa Cruz.

"I'm not sure," I say truthfully. "You?"

Quentin scoffs. "It's a bit late for me. I'll be forty in a few years."

"That's not old. Plenty of people, especially men, start families at that age."

He takes a big forkful of steak and chews it slowly.

"You didn't answer the question. Do you want kids?"

He takes his time with the steak before answering. "I was married to the military for so many years that I never thought I was missing out on anything. But I must be getting sentimental in my old age." He indicates the family in the booth. The man's got one of the kids on his lap, and he's laughing at something the kid's saying. "But when you see a family together like that…"

He doesn't need to finish the sentence; I know what he means. I feel it too, like maybe with the right person, under the right circumstances, it could be the best thing in the world.

"Why don't you want kids?" he asks.

"I never said I didn't want kids. Just that I'm not sure."

Quentin is friends with my father, and I don't want to say anything bad about my dad. He did the best he could under the circumstances. It was Mom who couldn't handle being a military wife. She admitted herself she was too young when they married, only eighteen. She didn't have time to experience any freedom or do anything for herself.

"If I was going to have kids . . ." I choose my words carefully, pushing the side salad around the plate with my fork. "I'd want to make sure I was ready. That I was living the life I wanted to live and that the man was all in on that."

My heart thunders in my chest, because for the first time I'm beginning to think I might have found the right man.

I dare a glance at Quentin, and he's staring at me intently.

"And are you living the life you want, Charlotte?"

My throat's suddenly dry, and I take a sip of Coke. How do I tell him that he's the one I want? That spending time with him makes me feel more like myself than any time in my life. That crossing the country on a bike on my own was damn scary and I'm glad I did it, but I'd rather do it with him by my side. I can't tell him that. So I make a joke instead.

"Going on crazy road trips with the world's biggest grump? I'm living the dream, baby."

Quentin sits back, and the moment's gone. We finish our meals and the singer, Dina, gets up on stage again.

We listen to her as we eat dessert, and I wonder if I'll ever find what I'm looking for. If I'll ever find my place to belong or a person I belong with. Or if I'll always be an outsider.

12

QUENTIN

I draw out the evening as long as possible, having a nightcap at the bar and chatting with Charlie.

Dina sings another set that's as haunting as the first. Sharon took the kids up to bed, leaving the man with the scowl to watch over his woman.

"I need my sleep." Charlie yawns and stretches. "We're up at zero-five-hundred right?"

I raise my eyebrows, impressed she's actually looked at the itinerary and has picked up on the correct way to communicate time. She's making an effort, and I like that.

"Afraid so. We need to find our spot and get set up."

She nods, resigned to the early start. "You better not snore."

I follow her up the stairs, trying not to watch her delicious ass, but it's no easier to get my eyes off it now than it has been for the last two days. By the time we get to the room I'm half hard, which is not a good situation.

I've unpacked my duffel bag already. My t-shirts hang in the wardrobe, my underwear is folded neatly in one of the drawers of the dresser, and I've tucked my duffle bag under the bed.

Charlie's oversized purse lays strewn across the bed with items spilling out of it. She wasn't joking when she said she travels light. I spy a couple of bunched up items of clothing and a toiletries bag. The rest is her makeup.

"You can use the bathroom first," I offer.

While she's in the bathroom, I pull out my laptop and check my emails. I confirm two meetings for tomorrow afternoon. This could be big for us, getting our beer distributed on the west coast, and I need to be alert. The last thing I need is to be distracted by Charlie. So when she comes out of the bathroom in nothing but a t-shirt, my jaw hits the floor.

I snap it shut and turn away, so she doesn't see the instant effect she has on me.

"I usually sleep naked," she confesses, which does nothing to help the tenting that's happening in my pants. "But for you I'll keep some layers on."

When I dare glance around, her eyes are dancing with amusement. This is all a game to Charlie. Probably because she has no idea what I'm thinking right now. If she knew I was in danger of ripping that t-shirt off and ravishing her, I bet she'd quit laughing about it.

"Don't bother," I say, and her eyes go wide before I can explain myself. "I'm not sleeping in the bed."

Disappointment flashes across her face. "Where will you sleep?" She indicates the room, which barely fits the double bed, a chest of drawers, and a wardrobe. It's a beautiful 19th century wooden design, but the space is limited.

"The bathtub." I grab a pillow from the bed.

Charlie laughs. "Are you serious? You can't sleep in the tub."

It won't be comfortable. But I've slept in worse places in the military.

"I can't sleep in the bed with you."

Her expression goes hard, and she looks away. I've offended her. And that's not what I meant to do. But Raiden will have my ass if I touch his daughter, and there's no way I can lie next to Charlie and not touch her.

She pulls the covers back and gets into the bed.

"You're a fool, Quentin," she says quietly. "But fine. Put your back out sleeping in the tub. I'm sure that's much better than finding out what might happen if you had the balls to sleep next to me."

I still at her words, and my breath hitches.

She feels it too. This attraction I have for her isn't one-sided. But the difference between us is Charlie acts on her impulses. I have the burden of thinking of consequences. And the consequences would be bad.

Raiden's my MC president, and we served together. It would be a betrayal. I'd be out of the club, which means giving up the brewery.

I'm not going to risk that for one night of passion. Even if my balls are so blue for this girl I might explode.

63

Besides, it's just not the right thing to do. I won't hit on Raiden's daughter.

"Goodnight Charlie," I say softly.

I grab the spare blanket from the wardrobe and head to the bathroom. I shut the door behind me and lean against it, breathing deeply.

If this is the right thing to do, then why does it feel so completely wrong?

13
CHARLIE

*T*he bathroom door creaks open, waking me up at some Godawful time. It's still dark out, and the inn is still and quiet. I squint at the flashing alarm clock by the side of the bed.

It flashes 4:59. My alarm goes off in one minute. But as usual Quentin is already up and ready to go. Screw him. I've got one more minute to stay in bed, and I'm going to take it.

I pull the pillow over my head, blocking out the sliver of light coming from the bathroom.

My head feels heavy, and I haven't had nearly enough sleep. I was worried about the idiot in the bathtub all night.

The fact that sleeping in a tub was a better option than sleeping in a warm comfy bed next to me shows how fucked up the sergeant is. He's in denial about what's between us, and it's driving me crazy.

We've been thrown together on this trip in a room

with only one bed. If that isn't a nudge from the universe, I don't know what is. My mother wasn't around as much as she could have been, but some of her hippy mindset rubbed off on me. Things happen for a reason, and being stuck together with only one bed when there's a fiery attraction between us seems like fate to me.

If an opportunity presents itself, you should go for it. And the growly ex-sergeant is the best opportunity I've had in a long time.

This is the perfect time to explore what's between us, but he's so far up his own ass he won't entertain the possibility. And now I've slept badly thinking about him all night, and I'm cross.

Beep beep beep,

The old school alarm clock blares near my head, and I jerk my neck up and fumble for the off switch.

"Morning."

Quentin is already dressed and shaved and looking as fresh as a new day. My head's banging, and I didn't even have anything to drink last night.

I scowl at him as frustration burbles up inside me. Frustration that he's dragged me across the country, frustration that he'd rather sleep in a tub than next to me, frustration that even at five o'clock in the morning, before my head catches up, my body is already responding to him.

My core tugs at the sight of him, and I long to pull him into the bed and rub myself against his hard muscles and find out what exactly it takes to make the ex-sergeant lose control.

But all that's impossible because he refuses to acknowledge that there might be something between us.

"I'll go find coffee."

He wisely exits the room, and I flop back onto the bed. With Quentin gone, I can get five more minutes of sleep.

Several snoozes, a grumpy Quentin, and a large coffee later, we finally leave the inn for the day. The festival is on the edge of town in an unused field.

Mobile vans and marquees are in neat rows across a wide grassy clearing. Towards the far end of the field, a stage is set up where local bands will play. Along one edge are the food trucks, already giving off delicious smells that remind me we haven't had breakfast.

The organizer directs us to our allotted area, which is right in the middle of the craft beers and opposite an organic wine stall.

Quentin parks the truck, and we get to work setting it up. The side pulls down to form a makeshift bar, and we bring out the stools and a few tables to create a small seating area out front. The fridges are attached to a generator, and we stock them up with our award-winning bottles. We've also bought kegs direct from the brewery which we hook up.

While I stock the fridges, Quentin heads off to get us some breakfast. He comes back with two breakfast burritos and a brown paper bag.

"For later," he mutters as he hands over the paper bag.

I open the bag to find a fat donut coated in thick pink frosting.

I'm touched he remembers that pink donuts are my favorite. I abandon the burrito and bite into the soft dough.

Quentin frowns. "You're supposed to save that for later. In case you get hungry when I'm at the meetings."

I chew the donut, enjoying the sweet sensation as it caresses my tastebuds.

"Why save the best stuff?" I say between mouthfuls. "If you want something, why wait?"

Quentin looks away and stomps off to check that the generator is cooling the fridges.

I notice him walking stiffly, and while he'll never admit it, I'm pretty sure that night in the tub has messed his back up. Silly man.

I finish the donut and get to work setting out the tasting samples on the counter.

By the time the gates open at eleven, we're ready to go.

The first hour goes smoothly. Quentin stays with me and we work well together, giving out samples and selling bottles of our award-winning beer to eager customers.

It's a different vibe down here compared to North Carolina. The men wear hipster beards neatly trimmed unlike the wild men back on the mountain. Not that Quentin would ever grow a beard. The military influence is too strong in him.

A couple of times, I catch him watching me when I'm

talking to male customers. He always seems closer, hanging over my shoulder whenever a young man talks too long with me, even though I'm only talking about the beer.

In the afternoon, Quentin heads off to his meetings and I manage the truck on my own. It's fun. I enjoy talking with customers, and we're selling well. I take a few big orders from local bars which we'll ship out from the brewery.

The story behind the beer brings in the customers as much as the award label. That it's brewed by veterans in a motorcycle club on the side of Wild Heart Mountain captures the imagination and makes people want to support us.

By the time the gates close at six and customers start drifting away, I'm exhausted. My body is weary from standing up all day, and I'm hungry.

We spend an hour cleaning up and restocking for tomorrow.

Today was busy but fun. Quentin's meetings went well. He brokered a deal with one of the biggest distributors on the west coast. Our mountain beer is going to be sold from Seattle to San Diego.

Quentin's humming, and it's infectious. I hum along with him and only halfway into the song realize it's one of his old man tunes. I guess his music isn't that bad after all.

14

QUENTIN

Charlie yawns over her lasagna, covering her mouth with the back of her hand.

"Sorry, what were you saying?"

Her eyeliner is smudged and there are dark circles under her eyes, but she smiles at me, her cheeks flushed from the success of the day.

We're back in the inn's dining room, too tired to try any other place for dinner.

Dina is singing again, and her tough-looking husband stands guard while the kids sit in the booth with Sharon and Vinny, their doting grandparents.

When I walked past for the restroom earlier, Dina was between songs, and I leaned over the piano to give her my compliments. Her husband strode over to us, glowering at me.

I backed off quickly. I guess the dude's protective of his wife.

It's the same feeling I had watching Charlie speak to

male customers today. The rational part of me knows it's her job to chat and be friendly, but the caveman in me wanted to drag her away and keep her hidden from sight.

She's gotten under my skin, and the more time I spend with her the stronger the feeling grows.

Now I watch her over the dinner table, animated despite the tiredness in her eyes.

We've been talking easily. The conversation always flows easily with Charlie, despite our age difference. It's like the fifteen years between us doesn't register to her.

"You're tired."

She nods. "It was a long day."

It's only nine o'clock but it's been a hard day, and we've got to do it all again tomorrow.

We finish up dinner without dessert, and I follow her to the room.

My back twinges when I see the bathtub. It still aches from the restless sleep I had last night, tossing and turning trying to get comfortable knowing Charlie was in the bed on the other side of the door.

Tonight after she brushes her teeth, Charlie closes the bathroom door behind her.

"I'm not letting you sleep in there tonight."

She leans against the bathroom door and folds her arms. I stare at the five foot something woman with the determined look on her face.

How can I sleep next to her and not kiss her or touch her?

She holds a hand up to stop my protest.

"I'll be asleep as soon as my head hits the pillow, Quentin, so I have no fear for my virtue."

She's right about that. I can see how tired she is.

The thought of another night in the tub makes my back twinge.

"Fine," I say, too tired to argue. "But stay on your side of the bed."

Her shoulders sag in relief, and she climbs into bed. I catch a glimpse of pale thigh which her t-shirt doesn't quite cover.

My heart rate goes up a notch, and as I climb in next to her, I wonder if this is a bad mistake.

But true to her word, Charlie rolls over to face the wall, and with her back to me her breathing deepens.

In moments she's fast asleep and I'm left staring at the ceiling with a massive boner too frightened to move in case I accidentally touch her and can't stop.

I wake to a warm body pressing into mine. Soft skin molds against my leg, and the scent of feminine perfume permeates my senses.

My dick lengthens before I know where I am.

Charlie's pressed against me; no, I'm pressed against her. My arm is thrown over her and her leg is draped over my thigh. Somehow in the night we gravitated toward each other and our limbs tangled.

I lie still, listening to her breathe. She's so close her every breath tickles my cheek. My dick stirs to life. It feels so right to have her in my arms.

But I said I wouldn't touch her.

I move my arm, trying to extract myself. Her breathing changes, and her eyes flicker open.

I freeze. The only light is the green glow from the alarm clock by the bed.

She's not wearing any makeup, and her eyes are dark pools. We stare at each other for a long moment. My heart hammers against my ribcage, and I should back off but I can't.

She looks vulnerable without her makeup. Raw and real. It's a gift to see her like this. The real Charlie.

She smiles faintly, and my eyes dart to her full lips only an inch from mine. Before I can stop myself, I lean into her. My lips brush against hers, and a zing of electricity sparks between us.

My eyes flick back to hers, and they're wide with anticipation. She's staring at me intently, like she can see into my very soul.

I kiss her again and this time she responds, her mouth moving against mine. Our bodies slide together, and the kiss deepens. I pull her toward me, needing to feel all of her, and she gasps when my hardness brushes against her belly.

My body aches for Charlie, and once I start kissing her, I can't stop. Her body is soft against my hardness. Her lips taste sweet and youthful against my dry ones.

Suddenly, I can't get enough of her. I grip her hips and pull her to me. It's been too long since I held a woman, and I've never wanted one as much as I want Charlie.

She moans, and the little sound makes my dick lengthen with need and longing.

I come up for air and she's panting hard, a line of perspiration on her brow. Her pink hair sticks to her cheek, and she's so beautiful my heart aches.

Without her makeup on, Charlie looks vulnerable and young. I pause. Because she is young. It's hard to remember when she's all made up with her leathers on strutting about with her big energy and confidence. But she's only twenty-two, and she's Raiden's daughter.

I can't do this. I can't take advantage of Raiden's daughter.

Summoning all the discipline of my military training, I pull away from Charlie. I untangle my limbs from hers and roll over onto my back, breathing hard.

Charlie props herself onto her elbow, and I can't look at her or I might kiss her again.

"What's stopping you, sergeant?"

She traces a finger down my chest. Thank God I put a t-shirt on going to bed. Even through the cotton, her touch scorches my skin.

I grab her finger to stop the torture.

"We can't do this." My voice is croaky, and I sounds feeble even to myself.

"Do what? Kiss or…" She leans over, and her warm breath skates my ear "…fuck?"

The word sends heat coursing through my body, and my hips jerk off the bed. I sit up, needing to get away from her before I do something we'll both regret.

"We can't do that, Charlie. You know as well as I do it's not right."

She sits up in bed and pulls the blankets around her. She's gone from playful to scowling, and I hate that I've done that to her.

"No Quentin. You think it's not right. I don't see what the problem is."

I stare at her, wondering how the hell she can't see that this is all wrong.

"Because you're fifteen years younger than me, because your father is my friend and the club president. I can't disrespect him like this."

Her frown deepens. "Why is that an obstacle? I'm not his property. I'm a woman, Quentin. I get to decide what I do with my life. My father has nothing whatsoever to do with my decisions."

I run my hands through my hair and grip the ends in frustration. Can't she see that this isn't how things are done? There's a code of honor, and sleeping with your friend's daughter is definitely not part of that.

"It's just not right."

I grab the pillow off the bed and the spare blanket from the closet. "I'll sleep in the tub."

I expect Charlie to admonish me, tell me off and get angry at me, but the look she gives me is sadness.

"If that's what you want, Quentin."

She's fed up and tired of me, and that's worse. She lives her life in the moment, but someone has to think about the consequences. And one night of passion could have grave consequences.

I head into the bathroom and try to get comfy in the tub.

15

CHARLIE

*M*y lips tingle with the memory of the kiss. Not just any kiss. When Quentin's lips touched mine, my body came alive in ways it never has before. And not just my body. When we connected with our limbs entwined and our lips locked, my very soul felt like it had come home.

I've never in my life experienced anything like the connection I have when I touch Quentin, which is why it's so maddening that he continues to deny it.

I don't understand his reasoning. Age is just a number to me. I don't care that there are fifteen years between us. I don't care that he's a friend of my father. Those things mean nothing when there's a connection like ours.

He needs to get over it and explore where this thing can take us. But I get it. He's fighting years of conditioning, years of doing the honorable thing. But there's nothing honorable in denying your feelings.

He just needs a little push to convince him to give this thing between us a shot.

Which is why I'm awake before my alarm goes off. It's dark outside and the hotel is still, but this morning I'm not hiding under my pillow. I'm up and out of bed as soon as I hear Quentin stirring in the bathroom.

The shower turns on, and I wait for a few moments before pulling back the covers and creeping across the floor.

Yesterday I slept until my alarm went off, and he'll assume I'm asleep now. But if I've timed it right, he'll be naked in the shower right about now.

With my heart hammering in my chest, I turn the handle to the bathroom door and push it open.

The faint glow from the screen of his phone is the only light. Quentin must not have wanted to risk waking me by turning the bathroom light on. There's a flutter in my chest at his thoughtfulness and it makes me bolder about doing what I'm about to do.

As silent as I can, I push open the door and slip into the bathroom.

He stands with his back to the door, water gushing over his muscular body. In the dim light I glimpse thick thighs, a perfect ass, and an inked back that ripples as he washes water over his face.

My breath hitches, and I forget to breathe. Heat floods my body and a sharp twinge tugs at my core. My panties dampen and my nipples stand to attention. He's perfection.

His hardened body turns, and his eyes widen in surprise as he sees me.

The words I had planned die in my throat. I was going to pretend I needed the bathroom, but that feels lame now that I'm caught in his gaze.

There's movement below his torso, and I look down to watch his manhood lengthen. His beautiful thick cock stands to attention and makes my pussy drip with need.

I lick my lips and swallow hard. My breathing goes shallow, and an overwhelming need to ride his thick cock makes me bold.

Before he has time to say anything, I step into the shower.

"What are you doing, Charlie?"

Quentin's voice has a word of warning to it. My t-shirt is immediately soaked with water and sticks to my breasts. His eyes glance down at my peaked nipples, and he takes in a sharp intake of breath.

"I'm doing what you won't."

I take his hand and plaster it to my chest, moving his fingers so they squeeze my needy breasts. He groans and I push forward, pressing my body against his.

"I want you, Quentin. I need you."

His eyes darken, and there's indecision on his face. I move his hand down my body and slide it between my legs.

He groans again, and the sound combined with his touch makes me shiver.

"I need a release that only you can give."

Quentin lets out a long shuddery breath. His hand

moves between my legs, and his touch makes me whimper.

"You're trouble, Charlotte." His voice is croaky, and the way he says my name is like a rough caress.

His lips find mine, and the passion in them tells me how much he wants this too.

He kisses me hard, and I respond with a feeling of triumph. He pushes me backwards until I hit the shower wall. I'm caught between the hardness of the tiles and the hardness of his body. I squirm into him, flexing my hips as his palm caresses me.

The water has my t-shirt completely soaked, but he doesn't stop to take it off. Instead he runs a hand underneath and up my body, and I arch my back as his fingers trail over my skin.

Every touch brings new heat to my body, which is made more sensitive by the hot water cascading over us.

Quentin hasn't shaved yet, and his stubble scratches my chin as he nuzzles my neck, kissing me behind the ears.

"Tell me what you need," he whispers into my ear, sending shivers down my body and into my core.

"I need you."

He groans at my words and grinds his hips into me. My hand runs down his taut chest and past the pubic bone until I grasp him in my hand.

"Charlie…" He groans as I stroke him, needing both my palms to cover the length.

His hand slides over my panties, and even through

the fabric, the sensation sends a shot of intense pleasure through me.

I cry out, and my head slams into the wall as my eyes roll backwards. One hand falls from his cock and with the other I squeeze him tight, not knowing what I'm doing any more.

"Tilt your hips forward," he commands.

I do as he says and am rewarded when his fingers circle my sensitive nub.

"You're going to come for me, Charlotte, like a good girl."

Even during this intimate moment, Quentin can't help giving commands. I like the way he orders me around in his gruff army sergeant voice.

One hand slides around my ass and grips it tight while the other explores my most intimate places. Although I've still got my panties on, the sensations are intense. I'd prefer there not to be a barrier between us, but at least he's touching me.

"Come for me, Charlie."

The pressure builds, and I grip him hard. "Don't worry about me. Focus on you, Charlie."

I do as I'm told, and with a final stroke the pressure breaks and I explode on his palm. Waves of pleasure and heat roll through my body, and I cling onto him as the orgasm shakes my world.

Intense sensations roll over my body, and for a moment I can't hear anything. Then the feel of water hitting my legs and the pounding of the shower against the tiles brings me back to earth.

When I open my eyes, Quentin's watching me intently. His hands are still pressing into my pussy, and he moves them slightly. A new pressure begins to build.

"You're beautiful, Charlotte."

No one's ever called me that before without my makeup on. And the intense way he's looking at me makes me think he means it.

His palm moves against me, and by now my panties are soaking wet from the shower and my own juices. I must look startled, because he looks concerned.

"Are you okay?"

"I've never done this before," I confess.

His eyes widen, and his hand stills. "You're a virgin?"

There were plenty of boys in the various towns where we lived in California who wanted to do it with me, but I never felt like I wanted to be close with any of them.

"I've never wanted to be intimate with anyone until I met you." He frowns, and a pang of uncertainty pierces my gut. "Is that a problem?"

He takes a few breaths and withdraws his hand from my panties. I shake my head quickly back and forth.

"Oh no you don't. We've started this, Quentin; we need to finish it."

"That was before I knew you were a virgin."

"What difference does that make?"

He runs a hand over his bristles. "It's big, Charlie. It's a big responsibility. Is that what you want? You think I'm the right candidate to lose your virginity to?"

I stare at him, uncomprehending. "Stop making a big deal out of everything, Quentin. I never met anyone I wanted to sleep with before. Then I spend two days in a van with you, and my body is acting like it's missing a limb and you're that limb. I want you. That's all there is to it. Don't over think it."

I reach for his cock, and he turns away.

"I can't do this, Charlie; it was a mistake. I won't be responsible for taking your virginity."

Anger flares in my belly. Why can't he see that there's something between us, and it's more than a quick fumble? I like him. I like him a lot. And now I've humiliated myself. I've thrown myself at a man who doesn't want me.

Tears of humiliation sting my eyes, and the last thing I want is for Quentin to see me cry.

"Fine." I step out of the shower and grab a towel from the rail. "You can live your life under a rock, Quentin, over thinking everything, but that's not how I live. I like you; I want you, and I know you feel it too. But you're too much of an ass to see it."

I fling open the door and head to the bedroom, slamming it shut behind me.

I thought we'd made progress, but the man's impossible. I thought there was something between us, and all he needed was a push in the right direction. But I was wrong. He's too set in his ways, and he won't ever change.

16

QUENTIN

The bathroom door slams behind Charlie, and my heart shudders with it. I had no idea this wild child was a virgin. I never would have touched her if I'd known. It's not right for a man my age to take something so special from her. She should be messing around with boys her own age.

The thought makes me clench my fists tight. I can't think about Charlie being with anyone else, yet it's impossible for me to give her what she wants.

Besides the age difference, Raiden would kill me if he knew I deflowered his little girl. It's just not right.

I ignore my aching hard-on and turn off the shower. By the time I'm dried and dressed, I'm ready to face Charlie.

She may not understand why this can't go any further, but she's coming at it from the perspective of a twenty-two-year-old. I've been around long enough to know you can't always get what you want in life.

Even if what you want feels so darn right.

Charlie is dressed when I emerge from the bathroom. She throws things into her bag without looking at me. Her body is tense and her shoulders rounded.

"Charlie…"

"Don't." She holds up a hand. "I don't want to hear it, Quentin."

She picks up her purse and dumps it on the floor, then busies herself with making the bed.

Her hair is wet and sticking to her cheeks, and she hasn't done her makeup yet. She's beautiful even when she's angry at me.

Desire fires inside me, and I resist the urge to cross the room and throw her on the bed. If things were different, if she were older, if she wasn't who she is, I could give in to my lust for her. If I was a different type of man, I would take her virginity and not care that we can't be together.

But I'm not that man. I won't give in to my selfish needs.

She looks so vulnerable bent over the bed with her hair still wet and her face makeup free. My heart aches for her. I want to cross the room and take her in my arms and say it can be different. But that would be a lie.

"We just can't get into anything, you know that."

She snorts and looks up at me. "No, that's something you're telling yourself, Quentin. But fine. You do you. I'm done."

She grabs her makeup bag and heads to the bathroom. As she passes me, I step back and clench my fists to stop myself from reaching out for her.

She misinterprets my movement, and her eyes flash in anger.

"Don't worry. I won't throw myself at you ever again."

"That's not..." But before I can finish my sentence, she closes the bathroom door behind her.

I've messed this up. Instead of apologizing, I've managed to make her even more angry with me.

I run my hand down my face and it catches on stubble. I haven't even shaved this morning. I never miss a shave. But we're out of time. It's another day at the festival, and I've got meetings.

While Charlie gets her face on, I head out to find us coffee.

There's a pastry shop across the road, and they're just putting out the first batch of warm donuts.

But as I bring the offering back to Charlie, I'm pretty sure even her favorite donut isn't going to mend things.

We barely speak as we set up the truck. I get us breakfast again and Charlie gives me a half smile, but the warmth has gone from her eyes.

She perks up as soon as the gates open and customers arrive. She's a natural at this, and I admire her ability to talk to anyone. Her confidence hasn't been diminished by me being an asshole this morning. She smiles and chats with everyone who visits our stall, speaking confidently about our product and upselling like a pro.

She's wasted working as a waitress in the restaurant. When we get back, I'll speak to Travis about offering her a job in sales with the brewery. She's got the personality and confidence for it, and her look fits the brand.

Her mood towards me softens as the day goes on. And I'm even granted a smile when I come back with a chicken burger for her lunch.

By the time I head off for my afternoon meetings, the tension between us has eased and we're talking together like before.

My afternoon meetings are a mixed bag. I sign on another distributor, and a couple of minor pub chains take preliminary orders.

But my mind's on Charlie. I haven't been able to stop thinking about her in the shower. How eager she was, how I made her dance on my palm. Then discovering she was a virgin. She's not the wild child she makes herself out to be.

I don't know if I did the right thing by pushing her away. I weighed the facts and made a split second decision that I'm sure is the right one for her. But it feels so darn wrong.

Perhaps when we get back we can spend some time together to see if this attraction is still between us. Maybe it will be different back on the mountain. Maybe I can take her out properly, spend time with her and get Raiden used to the idea. Or maybe she'll realize I'm too much of an old man for her.

When I get back from my meetings, Charlie is subdued and thoughtful. It's the last few hours of the festival, and the customers are dwindling. People are heading home, and some stalls are already packing up.

I catch Charlie leaning on the counter, chewing on the end of her nail as she stares out across the field.

"What you thinking about?"

She startles at my voice and shakes her head quickly. "Nothing." She grabs the last remaining bottles on the counter. "Can we pack up? There aren't many people left."

We work in silence, clearing the counter and tidying away supplies. We've completely sold out of the award-winning beer and only have a few bottles left of the others.

It's been a success all around and I should feel elated, but I only feel heavy as we pack up.

We drive in silence back to the hotel. I slide out of the van and head up the steps to the inn, but when I get to the door I realize Charlie isn't behind me.

She's standing by the truck holding her oversized purse in front of her. She carries the darn thing around with her everywhere.

"What time you want to eat? I'll book us a table."

She kicks at the gravel with her boot and doesn't respond. An uneasy feeling creeps into my gut, and I backtrack down the steps to get back to her.

"What is it?"

She looks up at me with a sad expression. "I'm not coming back with you, Quentin."

I frown at her, not understanding what she's saying. "What do you mean? For dinner?"

She shakes her head. "No. I'm not coming back to Wild Heart Mountain."

The heaviness in my stomach is so sudden it's like a punch to the gut. I reach out to steady myself on the side of the truck.

"You're not coming back to the mountain?" As if saying it again will make it any less true.

She bites her bottom lip. "No."

"But why not?"

She twists the handles of her purse, and I know before she says anything that it's because of me. Because I let this go too far, and now she feels like she has to leave.

"Don't go because of me, Charlie. I'm not worth that."

She gives me a sad smile. "It's not you, Quentin." She looks away when she says it. "I thought I might find something different on the mountain, but it's time to move on. And Santa Cruz is right there. I can get on a bus and be back at Mom's by morning."

I stare at her, the girl who biked on her own across the country to get away from California.

"But your stuff, your bike…?"

She shrugs. "I'll sell it to Mel. She's looking for a bike."

Mel is the most recent addition to the old ladies in our MC. The city girl had never been on a bike before she met Davis.

"But you love that bike." I can't comprehend how someone can decide on a whim to leave behind everything they own.

Charlie shrugs like it's no big deal. "It's only a bike. I'll buy another."

"But…" She can't leave. Charlie only moved to the mountain when her dad got married last year. She's got a job, and I thought she'd made friends on the mountain.

"How about your dad?"

"He's got his new family to keep him busy. I'll still visit, but we're both adults."

"At least come back and see him one more time and get your stuff, think about it for a bit."

She laughs, but it's a sad laugh. "I have thought about it, Quentin. I've thought about it all day. I hoped I'd find somewhere to belong on the mountain, but I was wrong. There's nothing there for me. It's time to move on. I've made my decision."

She shoulders her purse and steps toward me. "Goodbye Quentin." She kisses my cheek, and her breath sears my skin.

"But wait." I grab her arm and our eyes lock. This is when I should tell her to stay. But the words don't come. What can I say? That I can't be with her, but I don't want her to leave. Even I'm not that selfish.

She searches my face, but whatever it is she's looking for she doesn't find it.

I release her arm. "How will you get there."

"There's an overnight Greyhound that leaves from town in a few hours. By the time I wake up, I'll be in Santa Cruz."

A few hours. In a few hours she'll be gone. "At least

stay and have dinner." My voice sounds desperate, but I'm not ready to let her go.

Charlie shakes her head. "I'll grab a hotdog at the station."

"But…" I step forward and she cocks her head expectantly, waiting for me to say something. But there's nothing else to say. I can't ask her to stay. I can't offer her anything.

She smiles sadly. "I'll see you around."

Then she turns and walks aways. I watch her go, her thick boots crunching the gravel, her hips swaying and her shoulders back. The shock of pink hair bouncing with every determined step.

I watch the only woman I've ever had feelings for walk away.

But I need to let her go. Charlie will forget about me as she gets older. She'll find someone else, someone who can give her what she needs. I can't let my lust for her be a reason for her to stay.

It's the right thing to do.

Then why does my heart feel like it's had sixteen rounds fired into it?

17

QUENTIN

*A*s I watch Charlie walk away, my stomach feels like there's an arsenal of lead weighing it down. She strides down the street with her shoulders back and doesn't look back once. Then she turns the corner and she's gone.

I've spent enough time with Charlie to know that once she's made up her mind about something, that's it. She came to stay on the mountain on a whim, and now she's gone just as suddenly. How someone can live their life like that, I have no idea.

Maybe it's for the best. I can't think straight when Charlie's around. My emotions are all in turmoil. Not to mention what's happening with my dick. I've had a semi hard-on almost the entire trip with her, and it's been tough trying to hide it. Maybe it's for the best that she's gone. I can concentrate on the brewery and our expansion across the country.

With these thoughts swirling around my head, I head inside.

The inn is quiet tonight. The piano remains closed, and Dina and her little family is nowhere to be seen. I even miss her grumpy husband scowling at me.

The only other people in the restaurant is a table of two older men chewing on steaks.

The waitress takes my order, but when the food arrives, I can barely eat. I wonder what Charlie's having for her dinner and if she found a donut shop at the station.

I'm pushing the last of my fries around the plate when my phone buzzes. I grab it eagerly, hoping it's her, that she's changed her mind.

My heart sinks when it's only Raiden. He arrived back from Italy today and probably wants an update.

"Barrels. How's my girl?"

The knot in my stomach tightens. I rest my elbow on the table and press my palm into my forehead.

"She's good. She was good. She just left."

I brace myself for Raiden's anger. He trusted me to look after his little girl, and I ravished her in the shower and then let her go back to Santa Cruz on her own.

"What do you mean she left?" he growls.

There's no point beating around the bush.

"She's going back to Santa Cruz. Leaving on the overnight bus."

Raiden sighs. "I was worried that might happen, taking her across the country like that. I worried she might not want to come back."

He doesn't seem upset about it, just sad.

"She's a free spirit, that one. Goes where the wind takes her. I was hoping she'd stick around on the mountain. Charlie needs stability in her life, a strong hand. I wasn't there to do that when she was growing up. I admit I made mistakes with her. I was away so much on those long missions. I missed a lot of her growing up. She didn't get the discipline she needed. I won't make that mistake this time around."

Raiden's got a young family with his new wife. He gets a second chance, but that makes my heart ache for Charlie. Who's looking out for her? Who's being the safe place she desperately needs?

Raiden asks for an update on the festival, and I give him a run down. But I can't feel the enthusiasm I should for the deals that were made.

He tells me about his trip to Italy and meeting Isabella's distant relatives and visiting the mountain village her grandmother grew up in.

He tells me about travelling with a baby and a pregnant wife, and while he chuckles about the hardships of afternoon naps and diaper changes, I can't help feeling a pang of jealousy.

He's getting a second chance with a new family, and this time he's committed in a way he couldn't be when he was in the military.

He made that sacrifice when he went in, we all did, to put our country before family. It seemed noble at the time.

But when I think of Charlie, walking away with her

shoulders back, with no one to shield her from the world, my chest feels tight.

She's an independent spirit, but there's a vulnerable side to her. She must have felt like her father abandoned her when he was away so long on tours. And when her mother moved them across the country, by all accounts, apart from providing food and shelter, she left Charlie to her own devices.

Charlie may seem independent, but is that by choice or necessity? Am I just another person who has abandoned her?

Raiden's got a new family. He's found love. Why can't I have that too?

Something clicks inside of me.

The knot in my stomach works itself through my body until it gets to my head and finally gives my brain the message.

It's not just desire I feel for Charlie, although my desire for her is strong. So strong I've been blinded to my other feelings for her.

It's more than a physical attraction between us. I love her. I love that wild, crazy woman.

She knew it too. That's why she tried so hard to show me. I thought she wanted to give in to our attraction, but it's more than that and she knows it.

"I've been an ass."

Raiden stops speaking, and I have idea what he's been talking about.

"Sorry?"

"I gotta go."

I hang up on my club president and push my chair back.

Not giving into lust is discipline, but letting love walk out of your life is a sin.

"Add this to the room," I tell the waitress as I jog out of the inn.

I race down the steps. And jump into the truck.

18

CHARLIE

*G*reen Day blasts through my headphones. Damn, Quentin has gotten so into my head that I'm even into his music now.

The lyrics to "Good Riddance (Time of Your Life)" slice straight to my heart, and tears sting the corner of my eyes.

"Nope."

The woman in the seat next to me gives me a funny look, because yeah, I just said that out loud. But I will not cry any tears until this bus is on its way and I'm on the road away from here and away from whatever it was I thought I might have found with Quentin.

I wipe at my eyes and change the song. Slow guitar strings flood the headphones, and I skip that one too. I skip through ten songs before I find something that doesn't remind me of Quentin. I must download some upbeat shit for situations like this.

The bus driver throws the last bag in the underneath storage and closes it up. He climbs into the cab, and the bus doors wheeze shut. We'll be moving soon, and I can leave all this behind.

I'll go back to Mom's. Despite her faults, there's always a bed at her place for me. I'll get work at a diner and plan my next move. I've started again before; I can do it again now.

The thought of the Californian heat makes me tense. It's not a climate suited for bike leathers and heavy boots. I don't fit in there. I never have. I thought the mountains and Dad's MC club might be more my scene. And up until a few hours ago, I was enjoying myself.

But I'm not hanging around to watch Quentin do the honorable thing. Either he's too stupid to see what's between us, or he really is too much up his own ass.

He's a military man and they always put honor first, before anything or anyone else. I should have learned that from my father.

But I can't help the feelings I've developed for Quentin. How could I?

Thoughts of him has tears threatening my eyes again, and I clench my fists until my fingernails bite into my palms.

I will not cry.

I turn the music up and turn away from the window. The woman next to me gives me a small smile and I hate the pity in her eyes, like she knows I've been rejected.

I close my eyes, and with the sounds of Pink blaring in my headphones, the bus rolls out of town.

I must doze off, because I awake with a start as the bus jolts over a pothole.

There are murmurings from the passengers, and the woman next to me cranes her neck to see past me and out of the window.

I turn my head to see what everyone's looking at.

There's a small truck riding alongside the bus. Not just any truck. The outside says Wild Taste Brewery and the crazy man hanging out the window, one hand on the steering wheel, is Quentin.

"What the...?"

He sees me, and his look turns to relief. His window is down and he's saying something.

"Is he crazy?" the woman next to me says.

His head's sticking out the window, and he's keeping up with the bus. A car blasts its horn behind him trying to get past. "Yeah."

"Charlie..." His voice is swept off in the wind, and I can't hear the rest of his words.

"Is that you he's talking to, love?" the woman asks.

Either I left something behind or he has something to say. "Yeah. It is."

She looks excited. "You better open the window and see what he wants."

I stand up and pull the window open. It only opens a crack, and cool night air blasts into the bus.

"Charlie, don't go." Quentin says.

If that's all he's got to say, then I'm not interested. There's no point in staying if he's never going to act on what's between us. I scowl at him and shake my head.

I'm not shouting out of the bus to tell him I'm not leaving.

"I'm an ass," he says.

Which I don't disagree with.

"I love you. And I want to be with you. Don't go."

The scowl lifts from my face, and my heart stutters.

"What did you say?" I call out the window because I have to hear it again.

"I love you."

The woman next to me clasps her hands together. But it's the last part I need to hear him say again.

"And I want to be with you."

There it is. The promise that I need. I know he has feelings for me, but I have to know he's going to act on them.

"Tell the driver to pull over," he says. "You've got to get off the bus."

"Pull over!" the woman next to me calls to the driver. I spin in my chair, and she gives me a wink.

"Pull over!" a balding man a few seats down calls down to the front of the bus.

The call goes down the bus until it reaches the driver. He turns in his seat and scowls at me. But I'm already marching down the aisle with my purse over my shoulder.

He pulls off the highway onto the side of the road, muttering about timetables and late service.

"You'll need to get your own bag from below," the driver says.

"No need," I tell him. "I travel light."

He opens the door, and I step out into the cool night.

Quentin has pulled up behind, and as he marches over, the desperate look in his eyes tells me everything I need to know.

He grabs both my hands, and a zing of electricity travels up my body.

"Charlie, I've been an ass."

I nod my head. "Can't contradict you there."

"I was trying to do the right thing, but the right thing is to be with you. I thought it was only lust I felt for you, and I tried to fight it. But it's so much more than that."

He kisses my hands, scraping stubble over my palms.

"I love you, Charlotte. I love the way you don't take any nonsense; I love your confidence and your humor. I love the way you look without makeup, and that under your steel-capped boots you wear pink fluffy socks. Your music is… growing on me. I love your strength and independence, but most of all I love the way you make yourself vulnerable to me.

"I want to take care of you, Charlie. I want to be there for you, always. To be the person you can depend on who will never leave you. I love you, and I don't care what we have to do to be together."

There's a collective sigh behind me, and I spin around to find the passengers pressed up against the windows watching us. My seatmate has a tissue pressed to her eyes, and even the bus driver is hanging on every word.

"What do you say?" There's a wobble in his voice, and

I turn back to face Quentin. "Is it too late to give this a chance?"

His eyes search mine, and there's vulnerability in them too. Quentin's spent so long playing the army sergeant, always strong and dependable, rallying the men at the MC and turning their brewery into an award-winning countrywide business, that he's forgotten how to live for himself.

Maybe between the two of us we can find the middle ground.

My heart soars knowing this man wants me, not just physically but all of me. My brashness and independence and mood swings and spontaneity.

Maybe with him I can finally find a place to belong.

"It's not too late. I love you too."

His face lights up, and there's a cheer from the bus behind me. The tears I wouldn't let fall earlier trickle down my cheeks. But this time they're happy tears.

Tears because I've never stuck around before. I've never made myself vulnerable, and it's scary but also the best feeling in the world. Like I'm letting go of something.

Quentin wraps his arms around me and lifts me up into the air.

The bus passengers go crazy with whoops and cheers and clapping. I'm laughing as I turn around and signal to the bus driver.

"You can leave now. Thanks for waiting."

He dabs at the corner of his eye. "Good luck."

The doors whoosh shut behind me, and there's a blast of warm air on my neck as the bus pulls away.

Then it's just me and Quentin on the side of the highway.

His lips find mine, and this time when they crash into me there's no restraint, no holding back, only a warm feeling of belonging.

19

QUENTIN

The bus drives away down the highway with a final toot of its horn. But I hardly hear it over the thumping of my heart. I have Charlie in my arms, and that's all that matters.

Her warm body presses against mine, and I run my hands over her hips and up her back as I kiss the heck out of her.

She's soft and pliant, and my body responds to her with a desire so strong I can't help but grind into her, needing to feel her against me.

A car whizzes past and beeps its horn. I break away from Charlie, and she giggles. Her makeup is smudged with what I hope are happy tears, and I wipe one away with her thumb.

"Come on. Let's go back to the hotel."

I take her hand, but she resists my pull. When I turn back to her, a cheeky smile dances over her lips.

"Why wait?"

She steps toward me, and her hand slides over my chest. Her fingertips send heat coursing through me even through the t-shirt I'm wearing.

The backs of my thighs hit the front of the truck and she presses herself against me, crushing her body against mine.

My hands grab her hips, and even through the layers of clothes she feels amazing. Her fingers explore my chest until they hook under the bottom of my t-shirt. She starts to lift it up, and I put my hand up.

"Whoa, hold up. We can't do this here."

She fixes me with her cheeky smile, and her eyebrows rise in a challenge.

"Why not?"

I glance around us at the dark fields and the lights of the highway that stretch in both directions with cars speeding past.

"Because we're on the side of the road."

Even as I say it she grinds into me, and my dick pays attention. My pulse quickens at what she seems to be suggesting. Taking her right here, on the side of the road where anyone driving past could see us.

Charlie leans in until her warm breath grazes my ear. At the same time her fingers slide under my t-shirt, and her touch on my bare skin is like a blast of heat inside of me.

"Come on, sergeant," she whispers into my ear. "Live a little."

She nibbles at my earlobe and her fingers travel up

my torso and squeeze one nipple, sending new explosions of sensation through my body.

"Charlie…"

I can't resist her. I've held out for too long, and my defenses are weakened. But I'm not letting her seduce me. This time, I'm taking control.

I launch myself off the front of the truck, and she stumbles at the sudden move. I catch her in my arms and practically drag her around the side of the truck.

We're shielded here. No cars flying past will see what we're up to behind the truck, and there's nothing but dark fields in front of us.

I push her up against the side of the vehicle and run my hands down her leather-clad body.

"You want me to take you here on the side of the road?"

I nip at her throat as I say it, and she tilts her head back as a soft moan escapes her lips.

"Yes, Quentin."

My hand slides up the side of her breast, and I squeeze it through the leather. She responds with another moan that makes my dick twitch. But I hesitate.

"But it's your first time, Charlie. You should be on a bed with rose petals around you."

She chuckles her throaty laugh. "Stop over-thinking it, Quentin. It's what we both want."

As she says it, her hand snakes down my torso and squeezes my hard dick. There's no denying what I want. What we both want.

I should take her back to the hotel and make it sweet

for her. But she's leaning against the truck, her eyes dark with desire, breathless and needy.

Her hand slides over the bulge in my pants.

"Give in to your desires for once. Live in the moment."

She makes it sound so easy. And maybe it is.

I take a deep breath and let all the concern about doing the right thing go. Charlie's in front of me, and I want her. And I'm going to take her.

My dick stirs beneath her touch, and I kiss her hard. My hand snakes up the bare skin of her neck and I grasp her around the throat, kissing her roughly. She whimpers into my mouth, and when I pull away, we're both panting hard.

Slowly I unzip her leather jacket, exposing her pale chest and cleavage. I expect to find the cotton of a t-shirt, but when I unzip the jacket all the way, her breasts fall out, two bare orbs, the dusky nipples standing to attention.

She giggles at the astonished look on my face.

"You're not wearing anything under your jacket."

I can't take my eyes off her breasts. The nipples are perfect peaks that harden under my gaze.

"Have you been like this all day?"

"My t-shirt got wet," she says wryly.

A memory of the shower this morning flashes through my head and makes me twitch with desire.

"And the bra? Why aren't you wearing a bra?"

Charlie shrugs like it's no big deal. "I didn't bring a spare."

The thought of Charlie wearing nothing on top all day but her leather jacket makes my dick ache.

I can't resist anymore. I grasp one swollen nipple in my mouth and swirl my tongue around the hard peak.

She moans and I move my attention to the other nipple, loving the taste of her. Her hands tangle in my hair as I explore her glorious breasts with my mouth.

A car passes us by, and I barely notice. There's nothing in my awareness but the woman before me and the whimpers she makes as I caress her breasts, sucking each nipple into my mouth as my hands run over her skin.

I kiss down to her belly, and my fingers trace the outline of her leather pants.

"Please tell me you're wearing panties."

She chuckles. "You'll have to find out."

My hands tear at her zipper in my haste to see all of her. I want to touch every part of Charlie, to leave my mark and claim her as my own.

I undo the zipper and roll down the top of her leather pants. A flash of bright pink lace greets me. My heart races at the sight.

"Glad to see you brought spare panties."

She arches an eyebrow. "I'm not an animal."

I peel her trousers down and my hand slides around her butt, expecting to find the fabric of her panties, but instead I grab a handful of bare skin.

My breath hitches. My fingers trace the line of her panties, and I pull back to look at her.

"You're wearing a g-string."

A cheeky smile lights up her eyes. This woman's full of surprises, and I'm the lucky guy who gets to uncover them.

"Jesus Charlie…"

She's so perfect, and she doesn't even know it. My cock twitches with every new discovery, impatient to claim her. But I'm also enjoying unwrapping her.

"What other surprises have you got for me?"

"Why don't you find out?"

I kneel in front of her and peel her pants down her legs until they snag on her oversized boots.

"These need to come off."

I take my time undoing the laces. From down here I'm eye level with her pink lace-covered mound. The wind changes and her scent fills my nostrils, making my heartbeat faster.

I pull the first boot off, and she's got those damn fluffy pink socks on under her boots.

"You like the color pink."

She puts a finger to her lips. "Don't tell anyone. It might ruin my reputation as a badass."

I chuckle. She's making me laugh at the same time as driving me wild with desire. I can't believe how lucky I am to have found her.

I pull the second boot off and slide her leather pants down and off her feet.

I stand up and fold them neatly, and I'm about to open the door and place them in the passenger seat when Charlie grabs them off me and chucks them to the ground.

"They're only pants, Quentin," she says impatiently. "It doesn't matter if they get dirty."

She hitches her fingers under her panties and starts to pull them down, but I stop her hands.

"Oh no. Those stay on."

She's too sexy wearing nothing but her lacy underwear and the leather jacket hanging open. Even the fluffy socks look perfect on her.

I step back and catch my breath, admiring the woman before me.

"God you're beautiful, Charlie. Really fucking beautiful."

She smiles coyly. "Did you just swear?"

"I fucking did. That's what you do to me."

A breeze makes her shiver and I go to her, sliding my hands under her jacket and around her back.

"Hey," she says. "I'm not the only one getting naked here."

She gently pushes me back, and I almost stumble in the dark. She strides forward and hooks my t-shirt, pulling it over my head.

Her hands run over my torso, and I love the heat in her eyes. My muscles tense at her touch, making the ink or my tattoos dance in the shadows.

"You got any tattoos?" I ask. I haven't seen any on her.

"You'll have to find out for yourself."

Her hands reach for my belt buckle, and slowly she undoes me. My cock's sticking straight out, leaving a wet patch on my boxers.

I groan as she takes me between her palms, stroking

me from base to tip. If she keeps on like this I'm going to lose it, and I'm not ready for that yet.

I take her hands and pull her away from my throbbing cock. I push her roughly back against the side of the truck.

"Turn around."

My voice is tense, and her eyes widen. But I'm done playing games. I need to show this woman what she means to me and that I'm in charge here.

She does as she's told, spinning to face the side of the truck.

Her jacket covers her butt cheeks, and her thick thighs are tantalizing in the dim light.

"Put your hands against the van and spread your legs."

I expect resistance, but Charlie does as she's told.

The jackets rides up, and her perfect butt cheeks wink at me in the moonlight. A thin piece of pink lace nestles between them, framing them in the delicate fabric.

My heart hammers against my chest. She's perfection. Waiting for my command.

I chuckle. "I found your tattoo." On her left butt cheek there's a yin and yang symbol, perfectly round. It suits her to perfection. The hardness and the softness.

I trace it with my finger, and she gasps.

"You found *one* of them."

She throws me a look over her shoulder that's all sass. I'm going to wipe that cheeky look off her face.

My hand slides between her legs, and I cup her mound. It's warm in my hand and the lace tickles my skin. Charlie gasps, and her mouth pops open. I press my body behind her so my mouth is by her ear.

"You're going to stay like this with your hands up until I say you can move."

My hand strokes her through her panties, and they grow wet under my touch.

She whimpers, but I need more from her.

"What was that?"

"Yes."

"Yes what?"

"Yes, sergeant."

I reward her by sinking to my knees. My jeans are half off and my knees graze the ground. But I don't care. Down here, the scent of Charlie's arousal fills my senses and lends an urgency to what we're doing.

I run my fingers over her pussy, but I need to get in, to taste her.

"Tip your hips back."

She does as she's told, and I scoot around so that I'm sitting between her thighs. I slide in between her legs and kiss her soft thighs.

Charlie moans, and I pick up one of her legs and drop it over my shoulder. Then I slide the edge of her panties back with a finger.

But this woman has another surprise for me. Instead of springy hair, there's nothing but smooth skin under her panties.

My breath catches.

"Who did you do this for?" Jealousy surges in me, unrestrained and sudden.

Charlie gives a low chuckle.

"Relax. I did it for me. I like the feel of it when I touch myself. When I touch myself thinking about you."

Heat zings through my body imagining Charlie rubbing herself. My cock jerks, and I almost lose it.

This woman is too much.

I press my mouth to her bare mound and silence her with my tongue.

Charlie gives a yelp of surprise and her hips buck. I keep the pressure light, giving her time to get used to the sensation.

When I feel her relax, I grab her ass and pull her onto my tongue. She tastes like sweetness and life and leather, and I can't get enough.

My fingers sink into her soft butt cheeks, and I tilt her back and forth so she's riding my tongue.

"Quentin…"

She moans my name and it touches something in my chest, making me feel lighter and spurring me on. I'll do this every day for the rest of my life if only she'll moan my name like that.

The night breeze makes the hair on my exposed legs stand on end, but I need the chill air to calm my overheated body.

I use one finger to slide inside her and then another, getting her ready to take me.

Charlie finds her own rhythm as she slides over my tongue.

"Can I move my hands?" she asks, a plea in her voice.

I break away to tell her no. And instead she slams her fists against the side of the van.

"It's too much," she whines.

Then the orgasm claims her and she shouts my name into the wind as she explodes on my tongue, coating me with juices and nearly breaking my neck with the way her thighs clench around my head.

I crawl out from under her and pull her panties right off before spinning her around.

Her eyes are wide and dark, and for the first time Charlie is speechless. But we're not done yet. With her juices still flowing, I press her against the van and kiss her hard.

My dick nestles between her thighs and she parts them, letting me in.

"Quentin…" she whimpers when we break the kiss. "I didn't know it could feel that good."

She's looking at me with wide eyes like I'm a returning hero from battle, and my chest swells. I'll be her hero every day just to have her look at me like that.

"We haven't even gotten to the good part yet."

I slide my hand under her butt and lift one cheek up, lifting her leg and opening her thigh.

"You ready for this?"

She nods and presses her lips together. She's nervous, but she won't admit it.

My dick slides between her folds, and her head tilts back at the sensation. A hundred nerve endings spring to life and pre-cum shoots out of me, and I'm not even inside her yet.

I grab the base of my cock and guide it to her entrance.

A thought crosses my mind. "I don't have a condom."

Charlie shakes her head slowly, a smile on her face. "I don't care, Quentin. I want this, and I want it now."

I pause, breathing hard because I do too. But sex without a condom is irresponsible.

She leans forward and nibbles at my ear.

"Don't over think it, sergeant. Live in the moment for once. "As she leans forward her body presses against mine, causing the tip of my cock to slide inside her.

The sensation is immediate. Pure pleasure courses through my body, and I grip the base of my dick tight before it detonates.

My eyes squeeze shut, because if I look at the beautiful woman before me with her perfect breasts winking in the moonlight, then I'm going to lose it.

Charlie kisses my earlobe. "Do it, sergeant," she urges. "Make me your woman."

Damn the consequences. An image of Charlie, her belly swollen with my baby, flashes in my mind. And I like it.

If those are the consequences, then I'm all in. Suddenly I don't care that I might get her pregnant. I want to get her pregnant. I want this woman tied to me, with my children. I want a family with her, a future.

With a grunt, I thrust into Charlie. The warmth that envelopes me spreads through my body, and I don't just feel it in my dick but in my heart and in my very soul.

Charlie cries out and I pause, worried I've hurt her. Her face scrunches up, and she tenses.

"Look at me, baby. Open your eyes."

Her eyelids flick open, and we lock eyes. We're both breathing hard, and for a few heartbeats we stare at each other.

Another car goes by, and the breeze sends a ripple of cool air over my backside.

Charlie's shoulders relax, and her pussy releases its tight grip on me. Slowly, I move back and forward, finding the rhythm.

Another car passes, and the headlights bring her breasts into the light.

"You're beautiful, Charlotte."

I capture a nipple in my mouth, and she moans as I tease it with my tongue.

My hands grasp her hips and I brace my muscles, then lift her up. She gasps as the movement takes me deeper.

Then her thighs wrap around my hips. I push her against the truck, using it to take some of the weight and helping her to get the friction she needs.

We move together with the night surrounding us. The occasional whiz of a car passing sends a thrill through me every time.

Locked together, our bodies slam against each other as the pressure builds.

Charlie pants my name, and I don't care if anyone is out here to hear us. All I care about is the pleasure that's building in the base of my balls.

Then she explodes and her pussy tightens, and I can't hold back any longer.

I let go, finally. I let go of all the pent up desire I've been carrying for this woman, the challenges, the sassy remarks, the yearning for her.

It explodes out of me, and I let out a loud bellow that sends a flock of nesting birds out of the power lines above us and into the sky.

"Charlie!" I cry into the night as I release all my desire into her.

She sags against me, trembling, and I ease her to the ground, keeping my arms wrapped tightly around her.

My knees are gritty with dirt, my t-shirt torn, and I don't know where my underpants are.

But I don't care. I have my woman and my new mission in life. To take care of her and make her happy.

As we stumble into our clothes, there's a lightness in my chest I've never felt before.

I have Charlie, and I don't care about the consequences.

20
CHARLIE

*Q*uentin's hand tightens in mine as we cross the parking lot to the Wild Riders MC headquarters. My dad's bike is parked with the rest of the motorbikes which means he's inside.

We took three days on the return trip, making love in rundown motel rooms on the side of the highway. There were plenty of opportunities to tell my dad, but Quentin wants to do it in person.

So here we are. Back on Wild Heart Mountain, the truck parked in the parking lot and Quentin striding ahead with his hand firmly clasped in mine.

He's freshly shaved with a crisp t-shirt on, but there's a line of perspiration on his forehead, which is the only sign he's nervous.

I still don't know what he has to worry about. My father's not the boss of me. I was all for telling him over the phone about us, but Quentin insisted on speaking to him face to face.

We head to the bar first where Davis is polishing glasses. Luke has his wheelchair pushed up to a table where he's folding napkins.

"Thank God you're back," he says. "They took me out of the workshop to set tables."

Luke's still a prospect and has to go where he's asked, even if he is one the best bike mechanics in the shop.

Davis comes out from behind the bar and gives Luke a playful punch on the arm.

"And we missed you, Charlie."

His gaze drops to where my hand is locked with Quentin's, and his smile falters. "About damn time."

I startle in surprise. I've become friends with Davis since we work together so often, and I had no idea he had noticed the attraction between Quentin and me.

"Where's Raiden?" Quentin asks.

"He was in the office a minutes ago."

Quentin starts for the door, tugging me behind him.

"This is going to be interesting," mutters Davis. "Better get the popcorn on, Luke."

Quentin frowns at him and is about to say something when Dad strides into the room.

"You're back!"

The banter stops, and everyone pauses what they're doing. Quentin drops my hand, and the shock of the action makes me catch my breath.

Dad embraces me and shakes Quentin's hand, and they start talking about the roads and the journey back.

I stand there like a spare wheel wondering when Quentin's going to tell him.

119

The conversation turns to the festival and how we're going to fulfill all the new orders. I nibble on the end of my fingernail, waiting for Quentin to say something about us.

As their conversation drags on, my heart sinks. He's not going to say anything. When it comes to facing up to my dad, his stupid honor is going to get in the way after all.

I fold my arms and huff, and finally both men turn towards me.

"And how's my girl? Did he look after you on the road?"

A vision from our morning love-making session of Quentin's head between my thighs flashes into my head.

"He did."

I catch Quentin's eye, and he's staring at me with a soft look. His hand reaches for mine, and our finger entwine.

All my worries about him slip away, and we share a smile.

My father frowns, and his gaze drops to our entwined fingers.

"We've got something to tell you." Quentin's voice is steady, and he squeezes my hand.

"What the fuck?" My dad doesn't give him the chance to speak. "Why are you holding hands with my daughter?" His voice has a dangerous edge, and I take a step back. I've never seen Dad angry like this before.

But Quentin holds his ground.

"We're together."

"Like fuck you are." Dad pulls himself up straight and glowers at Quentin. "What did you do to my little girl?"

He pushes Quentin in the chest, and his hand is wrenched from mine as Quentin staggers backwards. He bumps into the table, sending the pile of napkins Luke was folding tumbling to the ground.

"Fuck," Luke mutters but wisely wheels himself out of the way and joins Davis by the bar.

Quentin holds his hands up in front of him in a placating gesture.

"I tried to fight it, but what's between us is too strong."

"You should have fought harder." Dad pushes him again, but Quentin won't fight back. "She's my fucking daughter. You had one job, Quentin, one job. Protect Charlie, look out for her, not…"

He turns away and runs a hand through his hair. "She's my fucking daughter!"

"She's right here," I cut in. "I'm twenty-two years old, Dad. I can make my own decisions."

He turns on me, and I've never seen him this angry. I cower backwards.

"You're vulnerable, Charlie. I wasn't around when I should have been, and your mother wasn't exactly there for you either. You're desperate for acceptance, and now you've fallen into the arms of the first man who offers you that. My so-called friend who should have known better."

He spits the last bit at Quentin.

His words make my head spin. Is that true? Am I falling for Quentin because he's the first man who's treated me right?

I glance at Quentin, and he's staring at me intently and he shakes his head softly. *No.* A rush of emotion cascades through me. It's more than that. I know it is.

"It's not like that, Dad."

"It's exactly like that, and he should have known better." His wrath turns to Quentin. "Get the fuck out of my club."

Quentin pulls himself up to his full height. "I'd hoped you of all people would understand about love." He's referring to my dad's second marriage to a much younger woman who he had no business falling for.

Quentin reaches out a hand to me. "Come on, Charlotte. Let's go."

I search my dad's face, because I don't want to leave like this. I want his blessing, and I want him to be happy for us. But all I see is anger and hurt.

I take Quentin's hand.

"If you leave with her, don't come back."

Quentin hesitates, and my heart is in my throat. When it comes down to it, he's not going to choose me. I try to slide my hand out of his. To let go before he can reject me. But he only clasps it tighter.

"I'm sorry you feel that way, Raiden. But I love Charlotte, and I'm not giving her up."

"You're just going to walk away?" Dad sounds incredulous even though that's just what he told Quentin to do.

"You're going to walk away from the club and the brewery and everything that that we've built together?"

Quentin looks at me. Our eyes lock, and his expression softens.

"Yes," he says simply.

Then he turns, and with his hand firmly in mine, heads for the door.

I stumble after him down the corridor and out into the fresh air. My emotions are in turmoil. This was supposed to be easy. I never meant to make him choose between me or the club.

"You can't leave the club, Quentin. You can't leave the brewery."

Tears are streaming down my cheeks, and he stops to wipe them away.

"I can and I will. You're the most important thing to me, Charlotte. Live for the moment, whatever the consequences, right?"

He's got a wild grin on his face, and his smile is infectious.

"So dry your eyes and grab your bike. We're getting out of here."

My pulse races as we cross the tarmac to where Colter parked our bikes in the workshop. I stuff my purse in the saddle bag and slide my helmet on.

The bike thrums to life underneath me, and I glance over at Quentin. My pulse is racing, and it picks up at the wild look in his eyes.

"Where to?"

He shrugs his shoulders, and there's a wide grin on

his face. "I don't know, baby. Let's just drive and see where the road takes us."

We rev our engines, and I follow him out of the parking lot and down the mountain road. The wind whips at my face as we leave the Wild Riders MC clubhouse behind us.

21

QUENTIN

Two weeks later...

*L*ate morning light steams through the window of the hotel as my eyes flicker open. A warm body presses against me, our limbs tangled in the sheets. The clock by the bed says it's almost zero-nine-hundred hours. I can't remember the last time I slept this late. Maybe it's because there wasn't a lot of sleeping happening last night.

We've spent the last few weeks exploring the seaside towns along the east coast, starting from North Carolina all the way to Miami. Sometimes stopping for two nights in a place we like, sometimes riding all day.

I have no idea where we'll end up or what we'll do when we get there. Charlie has taught me to live in the moment and not to think of the future. At some point we'll need to. But not yet.

I roll over and sling my arm over Charlie, and she stirs under me.

"Morning."

She grunts and rolls over, and I tuck myself into her body. She's warm and sleepy, and I catch the scent of her shampoo as I nuzzle into her neck. Even though I only intended to snuggle, my dick lengthens.

She senses it and pushes her hips back and into me.

"Someone's up and awake," she murmurs, grinding into my hardness.

I stroke her arm and plant kisses on her delicate skin. She tastes of sleepiness and sweat from our actions last night.

I slide my hand over her stomach and upwards to find her breasts. My hand cups the soft flesh, and she gasps as I flick a nipple.

"Are the girls awake yet?"

"They are now." Her voice is croaky and sexy in the morning, and it makes me want her even more.

I nibble behind her ear in the spot I've learned drives her nuts. She shudders against me and her body moves, pushing into me.

I pull the sheets out from where they're tangled around our legs. We're both naked, and I hook my leg over hers and slide forward. My cock nestles into the crevice between her butt cheeks, and the tip slips between her folds.

I groan at the heat and slickness it finds there. She's already wet for me.

Charlie reaches a hand between her legs, and she guides me into position. I nudge inside and her back arches. She tucks her legs up and pushes her hips back, helping me go deeper.

My fingers strum her nipples and I plant kisses on her neck, her back, every part of her I can reach. My two weeks growth scratches at her skin, but she tells me she likes it. The rough with the smooth.

Her hand stays between her legs, and she strokes herself as I thrust.

I take it slow, covering Charlie with kisses and working her into a frenzy until she comes undone.

When her climax subsides, I roll her over and climb on top. Her hair sticks up in pink spikes, and she's wearing no makeup. She hasn't worn any makeup since the day we rode off together. And I like it. I like seeing her like this, completely naked and sprawled on the bed. She's a vision.

"You're beautiful, Charlotte."

She smiles a sexy, lazy smile. "So are you."

I rise up above her and thrust deep inside. Her back arches as she takes me all in. I'll never get tired of this sight. Of Charlie before me, vulnerable and trusting.

Once inside I lean forward, wanting to be near her. Her breath grazes my lips, and our eyes lock.

"I love you."

Her eyes light up at the words and I thrust deep, my gaze never leaving hers.

"I love you too."

Our bodies move together in sync. We breathe together, and our hearts beat in tune.

When the pressure starts to build, I pull her hips upward, sending me deeper inside and providing more friction.

"Quentin…" She pants my name, and I can tell she's close.

"Come for me." At my words she falls apart, and I fall with her. My orgasm detonates through my body and into her, and I wonder if my aim will be true. If this is the time I'll plant a baby in her belly.

We lie together afterwards with her head on my chest and my arm around her. My fingertips idly stroke her hip.

"What do you want to do today?"

She gives me a cheeky smile, and her hand strays between my legs. "I can think of something."

It's another two hours before we're dressed and ready to leave the motel to look for lunch. We're about to head out when there's a knock on the motel door.

I pull it open and come face to face with Raiden.

I stiffen and step in front of the door, blocking him from entry. If he's come here to take Charlie back, then he'll have to get past me.

"What are you doing here?"

He looks grim, and there are dark lines under his

eyes. His gaze darts past me, and there's relief when he sees Charlie.

Raiden holds his hands up and takes a step back. "I'm not here to cause trouble. Can I come in?"

Charlie comes up behind me and slides her arm around my waist.

"Only if you behave."

Raiden nods and I step back from the door, eyeing him warily.

There's a small table opposite the bed with two chairs, and he takes a seat. I remain standing, and Charlie perches on the end of the bed.

"How did you find us?" I ask.

He looks at Charlie. "Don't be mad. Davis told me."

Charlie scowls. "Snitch," she mutters. The genial bartender was worried about her, and she's been staying in touch and letting him know we were okay.

"It's not his fault," Raiden says. "I can be pretty convincing when I want to be."

"What do you want?" I get to the point. "I'm not giving up Charlie, so you're wasting your breath if that's what you came for."

He huffs. "I know. You proved yourself there."

He makes a fist and taps the table with it. "It's a hard thing to give your little girl up to another man. I reacted badly, and I'm sorry."

I uncross my arms. It takes a strong man to admit when he's wrong, and I respect Raiden for that.

"I accept your apology, but it doesn't change anything. We're together now, and you need to get used to it."

He drums his fist on the table, and his gaze goes to Charlie. "Is he treating you right? Is he looking after you?"

"You men." She shakes her head and her eyes turn heavenward. "I can look after myself. We love each other. We're together. Get over it, Dad."

He smiles at her. "Same old Charlie."

"But yes," she mutters. "He's treating me right."

"Good. Because if I ever hear otherwise, I'll set my wife's family on you." It's not an idle threat. Isabella's the daughter of a mafia boss.

"That won't happen," I say.

Raiden lets out a long sigh, and his shoulders sag. He puts his elbow on the table and rests his forehead on his palm.

"I overreacted, and I said some things in the heat of the moment that I didn't mean."

I put my hands on my hips, waiting to hear where this is going.

He looks up at me, and he's no longer the wronged father but the friend I've known for the last ten years. The man I served beside, the man with the crazy idea to start a motorcycle club when we both found ourselves out of the institution we'd sworn our lives to.

"Will you come back?"

My chest lightens, and I steal a glance at Charlie. I poured my life into that club. That brewery's my baby, but I walked away from it for her, and I'd do it again if I have to. If she'd rather stay on the road and leave that all behind, then I will too.

She gives me a little nod, and my heart warms for her. She knows how much it means to me, and she won't make me choose.

"Only if you promise you're cool with me and Charlotte."

Raiden nods. "I promise."

Charlie stands and takes my hand. "Even if we decide to have a baby together."

Raiden runs a hand through his hair. "Jesus, are you…"

"No." She laughs. "But you have to be prepared Dad, because this is serious."

I put my arm around my girl and pull her to my side.

"Yes," he says. "I'm okay with it. Just please come back. The place is falling apart without you, and the guys are giving me death stares and calling me a hypocrite behind my back."

I chuckle and he laughs, and the last of the tension falls out of the room.

"I'll come back," I tell him. "But we're going to finish our road trip first."

"You'd better hurry, 'cause Kendra was having labor pains this morning."

"What?" The thought of my little sister having her baby without me has me reaching for my jacket.

"Relax," says Raiden. "They were the false ones. But I don't think that baby's going to go to full term."

"You ready to head back?" I ask Charlie.

She smiles up at me, and my heart warms. "You know me. I'll go wherever life takes me."

EPILOGUE

QUENTIN

Two Months Later…

"That's it…" Charlie moans as I turn my hips slightly to the left. Her thighs wrap around my back tighter, and I feel her heels digging into my kidneys.

Hot water cascades around us, and I tighten my hold on her ass as I slam into her. Her head hits the shower wall, and she grabs my shoulders and leans forward.

Her breasts bounce in my face, and I suck a hard nipple into my mouth.

She cries out and bucks forward, and I slam into her until she tenses against me. Her head jerks backwards, and she screams my name as she comes.

Not able to hold it together anymore, I bounce her on my cock until the release explodes out of me.

I cry her name over and over until my chest aches and there's nothing left in me.

My phone buzzes from where I left it on the vanity, but I ignore it. Instead I lower Charlie to the tiles and cover her face in soft kisses.

My phone rings insistently, and whoever wants to get ahold of me isn't giving up.

"I'd better get that."

I leave Charlie in the shower while I grab a towel and answer my phone.

"We're leaving in fifteen minutes. Are you guys joining us?" It's Judge, and he sounds pissed.

I glance at the wall clock, and it's zero-six-forty-five. We were meant to be at the headquarters fifteen minutes ago. It's the first day of the charity run, and we're heading out together. Breakfast was served at zero-six-hundred hours, which we've missed. The briefing was at zero-six-thirty, which we've also missed. Group photos are happening about now. And we roll out at zero-seven hundred.

Through the glass of the shower, I watch Charlie lather soap over her body.

"We had a hold up." She runs the soapy suds over her breasts, and my cock springs to life as if it hasn't just been drained. "Be there soon."

I hang up before Judge can say anything else.

"Are we late?' Charlie looks mildly concerned as I climb back into the shower.

"A little."

I grab her breasts in my hands and my mouth closes

133

over her left nipple, making her gasp. Somehow, being late doesn't bother me as much as it used to. Not when there are so many good reasons to lose track of time. And I'm holding two of them in my hand right now.

"Don't worry, we'll catch up."

I sink to my knees, and she moans as my mouth closes around her pussy. Her hand presses against the glass as she spreads her legs for me.

I'm late, but there's no place I'd rather be than right here living in the moment.

* * *

BONUS SCENE

Not ready to day goodbye to Quentin and Charlie? Find out what family life looks like when they settle down to family life.

Read the Wild Child bonus scene when you join the Sadie King email list.

To get the bonus scene visit:
authorsadieking.com/bonus-scenes

Already a subscriber? Check your last email for the link to access all the bonus content and free books.

ALSO MENTIONED IN THIS BOOK...

Curious about Dina the singer and her OTT protective hubby? Find out what obsessive behaviour Jaxon engaged in to win over Dina, and her mom in *Hot for the Cop*.

Jaxon

In my line of work, you see the worst of human nature, and that does something to a man. It hardens him, and it makes him mean.

I've done things I'm not proud of to protect the innocent of this city.

Then I hear her singing on the streets, her voice as sweet as an angel. It pierces my heart and tugs at my soul.

I'm a man of the law. I'm duty-bound to protect. But anyone who touches my angel will pay...

Dina

Mom's sickness has gotten worse, and we can't afford the meds. Every night I leave our tiny apartment to sing on the streets for cash.

When my money is stolen, I'm desperate. But how far will I go to get Mom the treatment she needs?

Hot for the Cop is an instalove age-gap romance. Sweet and steamy, it features an older alpha man and the curvy younger woman he claims as his own.

If you love BBW police romance books then *Hot for the Cop* is for you!

BOOKS & SERIES BY SADIE KING

Wild Heart Mountain

Military Heroes

Kobe brings together a group of military veterans who live on the side of Wild Heart Mountain. Can these wounded warriors find love or do their scars cut too deep?

Wild Riders MC

This group of ex-military bikers fall hard and fall fast when they encounter the curvy women who heal their hearts.

Knocked Up

A side story to the Wild Rider's MC. A secret baby romance featuring an ex-military demolition man who thinks he's not worthy of love.

Mountain Heroes

Steamy stories featuring the men and women from Wild Heart Mountain's Search and Rescue and Fire service.

Temptation

A damaged hero and a lost virgin in an explosive instalove retelling of the Hansel and Gretel story set in the woods of Wild Heart Mountain.

A Runaway Bride for Christmas

A snowstorm keeps this runaway bride trapped in the cabin of the mountain's biggest grump.

A Secret Baby for Christmas

Mr. Porter's Christmas takes a surprise turn when his daughter's best friend turns up with his baby.

Sunset Coast

Underground Crows MC

Short and steamy MC romance stories of obsessed men and curvy girls.

Sunset Security

A security firm run by ex-military men who become obsessed with their curvy girls.

His Christmas Obsession

A Christmas romance about an obsessed biker who rides across the country in the snow to reach Cleo before he's even met her.

Men of the Sea

Super short and steamy tales from Temptation Bay of bad boys and curvy girls.

Love and Obsession

A bad boy trilogy featuring a thief, a henchman and an ex-military hitman who finds redemption with his curvy girl.

His Big Book Stack

The Underground Crows are called in to help an old friend do some digging when the woman he's obsessed with is threatened.

Maple Springs

Small Town Sisters

Candy's Café

All the Single Dads

Men of Maple Mountain

All the Scars we Cannot See

What the Fudge (Christmas)

Fudge and the Firefighter (Christmas)

The Seal's Obsession

His Big Book Stack

For a full list of Sadie King's books check out her website

www.authorsadieking.com

ABOUT THE AUTHOR

Sadie King is a USA Today Best Selling Author of contemporary romance novellas.

She lives in New Zealand with her ex-military husband and raucous young son.

When she's not writing she loves catching waves with her son, running along the beach, and drinking good wine with a book in hand.

Keep in touch when you sign up for her newsletter. You'll snag yourself a free short romance and access to all the bonus content!

authorsadieking.com/bonus-scenes

Printed in Great Britain
by Amazon

52093517R10088